THE MISTWALKER

The Mist - Book 1

REGINE ABEL

COVER DESIGN BY
Regine Abel

ILLUSTRATIONS BY
Vvevelur
Artidoxx
Beth Gilbert

Copyright © 2018

CONTENTS

THE MISTWALKER

To be loved by a shadow in the Mist.

Every month, for three days, a mysterious fog filled with demonic creatures swallows the world. Since its first appearance a decade ago, I've diligently secured my home against the danger. Today, my sister's negligence has allowed something in. A Mistwalker. A part of him now resides inside of me, his brand on my chest a constant reminder of his presence. He terrifies me and threatens to derail the life I've been building. And yet, a part of me is drawn to him...

I have walked two worlds to be with her.

For years, I have lurked in the Mist, lying in wait for the opportunity to get to my fiery Jade. Now that humans have torn the Veil, nothing will keep me from crossing into the Mortal Plane to claim her. She's my mate. I will not allow her to hide from the truth she knows deep within her but fears to acknowledge. I was made for her. I am her greatest wish.

DEDICATION

To those who dare to dream, dare to take chances, and are not afraid to flip the bird at naysayers and conformists. Everything is possible if you wish it hard enough...

...and then work your tail off to make it happen.

CHAPTER 1
JADE

The civil defense sirens resonated in the distance, and the familiar queasiness settled in the pit of my stomach. Jumping out of the comfortable leather lazy boy I'd been reading in, I tossed my book onto the glass surface of the coffee table. Despite having verified twice already that the house was under proper lock down, when the Mist rose, you could never be too cautious.

After checking the reinforced front door and the window shutters of the entrance hall, I tugged at the metal shutters in the living room, testing the locks, then moved to the kitchen. Perched on a tall stool at the breakfast counter, my baby sister Laura was still babbling away on her phone. She absentmindedly stirred her coffee, which had, no doubt, cooled forever ago.

"Laura, I need you to go double check the windows in the bedrooms and bathrooms upstairs," I said over my shoulder while heading towards the kitchen windows.

"I'm on the phone," she grumbled, irritated.

I paused, turned, and gave her a disbelieving look.

"For fuck's sake," she said, "you've already checked twice!"

"NOW, Laura!"

She huffed and jumped off the stool, stomping her feet as she headed upstairs.

Biting my tongue in anger, I cycled through the kitchen windows and patio door. Of all the times to pay me a visit, Laura had chosen the start of the Mist. Despite her twenty-two years of age, she remained steadfast in her immaturity. And yet, she was rocking medical school like nobody's business. An honor roll student, she's earned herself one scholarship after another, allowing her to pursue the studies we couldn't have afforded otherwise. Orphaned at an early age, we'd been shuffled around from one relative to another until I turned eighteen ten years ago and took on the responsibility of my little sister.

In spite of her carelessness regarding her personal safety, the university's security ensured that all of the students were accounted for and the dormitories properly secured for the three days of the Mist. It did wonders for my peace of mind, knowing someone reliable made sure she didn't fall asleep with an open window.

Most homes and businesses had automated lockdown systems. I couldn't afford one yet, but in a few months, these shutters would get a significant upgrade. Entering my office at the back of the house—which also served as my painting studio —I made a quick round, already knowing everything would be in order. I closed the thick, off-white curtains over the metal shutters to give the space the illusion of normalcy and turned around to leave.

"JAAAAADE!"

I squealed in fear, my heart lurching in my chest before a sense of dread descended upon me.

"JAAAADE!" Laura screamed again from upstairs.

The terror in her voice turned my blood to ice. I raced out of my office, down the hallway to the stairs, which I climbed two at a time. As I reached the landing, white plumes of the Mist slithered on the floor from Laura's bedroom into the corridor.

No! No! No! Oh God, no!

Running the short distance to the room, I burst inside to find the shutters up, the guillotine window ajar, and Laura frantically trying to open the rotating lock at the top of the window. The Mist poured in through the three-inch opening below, spilling onto the floor like dry ice smoke. I'd never seen the Mist with my own eyes before, let alone felt its wet coldness against my skin. And yet, it wasn't the thick, whitish curtain of fog outside that caught my eyes and liquefied my innards, stopping me dead in my tracks, but the shadowy figure floating in the air, a few meters away from the house.

Its glowing, yellow eyes, previously trained upon my sister, shifted towards me the minute I entered the room. The wraith-like silhouette, barely opaque at first, suddenly seemed to solidify, the yellow glow intensifying as it stared all the way into the depths of my soul.

We moved at the same time, rushing towards the window.

"Run!" I shouted, shoving my sister out of the way.

The antiquated window lock needed to be handled in a specific way when it got stuck. Despite the terror choking me, I successfully unlocked the window in the first attempt but it hadn't been fast enough. The shadow wraith closed the distance at lightning speed, its dark, vaporous hand shooting through the opening to wrap around my left forearm. I screeched and shoved the unlocked window down with such force it surprised me that the glass didn't shatter. It severed the arm of the Mistwalker, but the dark smoke of his hand didn't evaporate; it spread along my forearm before seeping into my flesh. A thousand icy shards pricked me where the smoke had touched me then ran through my veins and up my arm before stabbing me in the heart.

My knees nearly buckled, and my breath caught in my throat. Leaning on the windowsill for support, my eyes locked with the glowing yellow ones of the creature. Despite its indistinct features, I recognized a mouth stretching into a victorious smile.

It rested both its hands on the window—the severed one having regrown—and pushed up. When the window began to reopen, I slammed it back down and locked it, realizing I had forgotten to do so, too shocked by the pain of the dark smoke entering my body.

The Mistwalker's smile broadened.

"You are mine, now, beautiful Jade."

The disembodied voice echoed in my head, sultry like that of a lover, and full of promises. My skin erupted in goosebumps in response to the undeniable connection I felt with the creature.

It knows my name!

But worse still, part of it now resided inside of me.

"Soon, we'll be together."

"Never," I whispered. "NEVER!"

Its taunting laughter echoed in my head, soon drowned out by the banshee scream of a nearby Mistbeast. He looked over his shoulder then back at me.

"Soon, my Jade. For now, I hunt."

He turned and flew away, quickly swallowed by the thick Mist.

Hands shaking, I closed and locked the metal shutters, refusing to draw the attention of the other dark silhouettes of whatever demonic creatures lurked in the nightmarish fog.

I wanted to curl up on my bed and cry, but other access points could have been left ajar. As soon as I opened my bedroom door, Laura shot to her feet and screamed from the corner where she'd been sitting, a letter opener clutched in her hands.

A million horrible words crossed my mind, burning my tongue, but I swallowed them and gave her an angry, disgusted stare that spoke volumes. Without a word, I checked my windows which I had known to be locked, then the bathroom, and moved on to the guest room also properly secured.

Laura shadowed me, sniffling and stuttering apologies I

didn't want to hear. Stomping past her, I headed for her bedroom. She followed in my wake like a scared puppy.

"Please, talk to me," Laura pleaded, wiping her tears with her sleeve. "Please, Jade. I'm so sorry."

I threw her pillows to the middle of the comforter on her bed then marched to the linen closet in the hallway. I pulled out a couple of towels, which I carried back to the bedroom and tossed on top of the pillows.

"What are you doing, Jade?" Laura asked, fear and confusion creeping into her voice.

"Grab your stuff," I said, my voice clipped. "You're spending the rest of the Mist in the panic room."

"What?" she asked, disbelieving. She stared at me, mouth agape, as I bundled up her blankets and pillows. "Fine, I messed up pretty badly, but you can't just lock me up in the basement like some naughty child!"

"Sorry?! You think you're fucking sorry?" I shouted. "I want to strangle you right now. You had ONE fucking thing to do and that was making sure your damn window was closed! But no, you were too damn obsessed with that goddamn phone of yours," I snapped while pointing an angry finger at the device still clutched in her hand. "You're so fucking irresponsible, and you had the nerve to give me attitude when I asked you to double check. You almost got us both killed."

Laura cringed and shrank into herself with each of my scathing words. I felt horrible tearing into my sister like that. Despite her many shortcomings, I'd never lost my shit like this, but terror still coursed through my blood, along with part of that Mistwalker.

"And you intend to be a doctor?" I spat out, immediately regretting it. Fear made me ugly.

She flinched, but that stung her into fighting back.

"That's a low blow," she hissed. "I already apologized. What the fuck more do you want me to do? I messed up, but now it's done! You're not throwing me in that stupid panic room."

"I wish it were done, *baby sister*," I said with sarcasm. "Except your little 'mess up' might still kill me."

She stiffened, her blossoming anger shifting to worry.

"The Mistwalker that was staring you down touched me before I could close the window. A part of him got inside me through my skin. Do you understand?" I said angrily, before hugging myself. "I can feel it in my veins. God only knows what the hell it might be doing to me. So yes, Laura, your ass is going down to the panic room because it locks from the inside. If *I* go down there and turn into some monstrosity because of this shit inside of me, I'll be able to walk right out and hunt you. But if you're downstairs, I won't be able to get to you."

Laura stared at me with a mixture of guilt, horror, and fear. I blinked to stem the tears that threatened to surface.

"Oh Jade... I'm... I'm..."

"Save it," I said, interrupting her. If I didn't keep moving, I'd fall apart. There'd be plenty of time to wallow in self-pity once Laura was safely locked downstairs. "Grab your stuff, make it quick."

Swallowing past the lump in my throat, I grabbed the bundle and walked out of the room. I ran down the stairs and opened the door to the closet beneath. The clever pattern on the wooden floor boards hid the trapdoor. Pressing the right section of the pattern with the tip of my foot opened the trapdoor, which folded up against the wall. I slid the metal panel to the side, revealing the wide staircase to the panic room. Hugging the bundle to my chest, I went down.

This room had convinced me to buy the house. While it had been poorly decorated, furnished for function over comfort, it possessed a titanium metal plate door to block access from above and a state-of-the-art ventilation system. One could hunker down for weeks down here and be safe. I'd revamped it since acquiring the place, adding divisions for two private bedrooms, painted it in bright colors, with comfortable carpets, couches, a large screen TV, a huge library of movies, and a tablet with hundreds of digital books. Thankfully, as with every Mist, I had taken the time to fully restock the small kitchen, just in case.

Halfway through making up Laura's bed, her light footsteps on the stairs resonated outside the room.

"Over here," I shouted while fluffing the pillows.

Complying, she made her way to the bedroom and advanced timidly inside. These few minutes alone had allowed my anger and distress to abate a little. The sorrow and guilt in the doll-like eyes of my baby sister tugged at my heart. I wanted to go to Laura, kiss her pixie face, and fluff her short strawberry blond hair. She'd hug me, and I would tell her that everything would be alright.

But I didn't dare.

What if I infected her with what had gotten inside me? Even now, I could feel the alien energy thrumming within, claiming me.

"You get to sample the new mattress first," I said, trying to lighten the mood.

Her eyes misted. "I'm so sorry, Jade. How do we fix it? I can't lose you."

My throat tightened, and tears pricked my eyes. "I know you are, hun. I'm sorry for yelling. This whole thing has me so freaked out, but it's going to be fine," I said with a forced smile. "It's only three days. We can text and call each other. Heck, I'll even use one of those video chat programs you like so much." Tears trickled down her cheeks, and her lips trembled, making it even harder for me to remain stoic. "I'm sure that everything will be fine, but we can't take chances. I love you too much."

"I love you, too," she said in a choked voice.

Laura took a step forward before stopping, understanding even better than I the risks of transmission. My arms ached with the need to hug my sister. Despite our differences, we were extremely close. We'd only had each other since our parents' untimely passing.

"Check if you have everything you need," I said. "You'll be pleased to know there's rum raisin ice cream in the freezer, and ketchup chips in the pantry."

She snorted and smiled through her tears.

I exited the room, and she followed at a safe distance.

"You remember how everything works?" I asked. She nodded and then hugged herself as I had done earlier. As a social butterfly, Laura would struggle with spending three entire days on her own. "It will be over quickly," I said, trying to sound optimistic. "Now is the perfect time for you to binge watch those silly TV series you enjoy so much."

I climbed the stairs and stopped at the top to look down at Laura.

"As soon as I'm out, you seal this place shut. Do not open to anyone, not even me, no matter what I say, until the city sirens go off, signaling the end of the Mist."

She nodded, tears building up again. "Okay."

"I love you, kiddo. See you soon."

"I love you, too, Jade. See ya."

I winked at her then exited the panic room. Seconds later, the thick titanium plate settled into place, covering the hole. With a painful sigh, I slid the metal panel above it then lowered the wooden door over it.

Feeling twice my twenty-eight years, I climbed the stairs to my bedroom with heavy steps. Since the Mist first appeared, I'd been diligent—borderline paranoid—about securing my place of residence to avoid becoming a statistic. But now, he was inside me, a dull, throbbing pain, just above my heart, that had been intensifying over the past few minutes. I didn't want to believe that something bad would happen to me, but the uncertainty, the not knowing, would drive me insane.

S oft hands roamed over my naked skin, caressing the curve of my shoulders before closing in on my breasts. I arched my back, pressing into the gentle touch as it teased my hardening nipples. Pursuing their journey south, my lover's palms skimmed over my stomach, diverged to my hips and down the length of my thighs before hooking behind my knees to spread my legs open. Cold air fanned over my slit before a cool tongue began to lap at me.

I gasped, as much with pleasure as with fear. My eyes snapped open. Instead of the familiar décor of my bedroom, I saw an endless void swirling with Mist. My lips parted to scream but a moan escaped me instead as my lover's tongue stabbed into my core. Impossibly long and thick, it darted in and out of me, flooding me with waves of sinful pleasure. Dark, vaporous tendrils wrapped around me, caressing, exploring, setting my skin on fire despite their cool feel. My mind shouted for me to pull away, resist, fight, but my body fully surrendered to the sensuous and oddly familiar assault.

"Come for me, my Jade."

I wanted to say no, yell at him to release me, but my body complied, detonating with earth shattering violence. Boneless, shaking with voluptuous tremors, I let myself float on the endless brume.

The Mistwalker passed through me, as one would walk through showering water. For an instant, we were one, his emotions seeping through me: victory, possession, and insatiable desire. I shuddered, torn between fear and an irrational excitement. The Mistwalker's dark, ethereal form rose out of my body and settled over me, his featureless face inches from mine and glowing, yellow eyes hypnotizing me.

"Cast away your fears, my Jade." His disembodied voice

spoke into my head. *"I will never harm you. Only give you joy and pleasure."*

Those words didn't reassure me. As the sensual haze of my climax dissipated, the sense of doom returned with a vengeance, and yet I felt in no immediate danger.

"Please, let me go," I begged.

"We belong together. I can't let you go. I won't."

"Why?" I asked, feeling trapped and helpless.

His vaporous hand caressed my cheek, then my lips.

"Because you don't want me to."

I gaped at him, speechless. That made no sense.

The barely visible line of his mouth stretched into an amused smile. He lowered his head and licked the skin right above my heart in an almost reverent fashion.

"Soon, all will be clear, my Jade. And then we'll be together, for eternity and beyond."

Before I could ask another question, a falling sensation startled me. I seemed to land heavily into my own body, then jerked into a sitting position to find myself safe in my own bed. The movement activated the motion-sensor of the night light. My eyes flicked to the metal shutters on the window. Finding them still properly closed, and the absence of Mist swirling around the room confirmed that this 'encounter' had either been a dream or some kind of out of body experience.

Taking stock of myself, and in spite of the lingering arousal, I had to admit that my body had not been touched; all of this had happened in my head. Relief flooded me. To my shame, I'd been a 'reluctantly willing' participant. But at least, I could shirk all responsibility by calling it a nightmare or twisted fantasy induced by my earlier traumatic experience.

Rubbing my chest where the Mistwalker had licked it, I winced at the tenderness. It still throbbed, and I had no doubt that was where his essence had nested inside me. Lying back down, I closed my eyes, hoping for pleasant rainbow and unicorn dreams, but sleep eluded me. Turning to my side, I stared at the shutters, wondering about the Mist beyond.

No one knew what had caused it, although everyone suspected our governments had had a hand in it. Nine years ago, on March twenty-sixth, a little after 8:00 PM, tearing, thunderous sounds had been followed by a series of bright lights that had flashed throughout every city around the globe. People called it a tear in the Veil between our dimension and another. From these rifts, a thick fog had poured out endlessly, swallowing the world, and bringing with it countless nightmarish creatures. In the three days it lasted, millions of people vanished, never to be seen again.

We had divided the Mist dwellers into two categories: the Walkers and the Beasts. While no one had survived exposure to the Mist to tell what lurked within, when it withdrew after three days, the dwellers that hadn't made it back to their dimension when the portals closed died, leaving ashy statues of their former selves. We didn't know if the sun, the air or something else caused it, but it fit the lore of vampires exposed to daylight.

I couldn't quite say why we called them Walkers as they didn't have legs but instead looked like faceless, shadowy wraiths with human-like arms and hands. The statues of the beasts greatly varied in shape and size, from small fox-sized creatures to building-tall, hulking, nightmarish monstrosities. However, the slightest touch or gust of wind sufficed to bring down those ash 'sculptures,' to use the term loosely.

Oddly enough, the Mist dwellers never tried to break into houses. They would try to open doors and windows but finding them locked proved to be enough of a deterrent. The Mistbeasts never attacked the houses. From all accounts, they merely lumbered about, looking for easy prey. Thank God for that, too. No houses could have survived an assault from most of these creatures. That behavior further emulated vampire lore according to which they couldn't enter your house without an express invitation. It made me wonder if they were bloodsuckers, too.

The population looked for someone to blame. But every country around the world being hit by the Mist, on the same day and at the same time, made it impossible to pinpoint a culprit. Conspiracy theorists spoke of government experiments, further supporting that theory with the fact that the Mist only rose with the full moon and faded after 72 hours, like a scheduled test gone wrong. For their part, environmentalists claimed our abuse of Mother Earth had unleashed something that would have otherwise remained dormant.

Indigenous tribes, homeless people, animal farmers and breeders, zoos and wildlife parks were the most severely affected. Many tribes completely disappeared over night, entire herds were decimated. However, construction companies enjoyed an insane boom in business, which still continued today with new improvements to home security against the Mist, automated lockdown systems, panic rooms, herd shelters, you name it. Needless to say, vegetarians rejoiced as the price of meat skyrocketed, forcing many to significantly reduce or eliminate it from their diet.

The screech of a Mistbeast outside, followed by the flapping sound of giant wings, startled me. A series of horrible scenarios I'd been trying to silence crawled back to the forefront of my thoughts.

What if I turn into one of those nightmarish creatures?

Yet, I dismissed that thought as soon as it entered my mind. For some reason, I totally doubted whatever lurked inside me would turn me into a Mistbeast. But the Mistwalker's words made me believe I might become like him. He'd claimed me as his and stated that soon we would be together for eternity and beyond. What else could it be?

I shuddered, anxiety driving sleep even further away. Every instinct told me this had not been a dream. It had felt too real.

Hopping out of bed, I grabbed my laptop from the small desk by the window. Settling back in my bed, legs crossed and a few pillows stacked behind my back, I fired up my device. After opening a web browser in incognito mode, I searched every keyword combination that might yield results for being touched by a Mistwalker.

Aside from a creepily official looking website urging people who came into contact with a Mistwalker to report immediately to the nearest Center for Disease Control—which I really didn't want to do except as a last resort—every other site belonged to psycho-groupies wanting to be taken by a Walker and have Mist babies. For a while, Mist pacts had become a thing amidst young, troubled teens, and yet another risk parents were asked to keep an eye out for. Small towns with little career prospects were severely affected, although the most dreadful case occurred in a big town where half of the local football team and two-thirds of their cheerleading squad walked out of their dorms and into the Mist.

My research yielding nothing, I tossed my laptop aside in disgust and watched it bounce on my queen-sized bed. With a frustrated sigh, I lay back down, weighing my options.

Thanks to video call technology, my sister would be able to see whether or not I'd turned into a monster by the time the Mist lifted. She'd then be able to call the CDC to come dispose of me. However, that sounded as horrible a fate as what I suspected would happen to me if I just turned myself in for having been 'infected' by a Mistwalker. But what if I did become something deadly? I always thought I'd be socially responsible if I ever found myself in this kind of predicament, yet right now, my survival instincts dominated. The thought of becoming a lab rat scared me even more than what the Mistwalker's essence inside me could do.

Why am I dwelling on this?

Why indeed. In truth, within seconds of him touching me,

when his dark mist entered my body, I'd already decided what to do if I turned. With my sister safely tucked away in the panic room, I'd open the front door of the house and walk into the Mist.

Strangely enough, consciously acknowledging this less than comforting thought lifted a heavy weight off my shoulders. My anxiety abated and my eyelids grew heavy. I touched the throbbing pain above my heart one last time before sleep claimed me.

CHAPTER 2
JADE

The tantalizing aroma of bacon, hash browns, and freshly brewed coffee stirred me from my slumber. Mouth watering, stomach rumbling, I jumped out of bed and ran to the bathroom to wash the sleep from my face. Laura was a fabulous cook and her hash browns could qualify as fine dining. She knew how much I loved them and never failed to make some for me whenever she visited.

As I turned on the faucet to wash my face, I looked up at the mirror, a nagging sense of unease at the back of my mind. My gaze never reached my face in the reflection, remaining stuck on the dark, cabalistic symbol which had appeared on my chest, above the lacy line of my silk teddy. Memories of last night's events crashed into me. I clasped my hand over my heart. The throbbing pain had gone. I rubbed the mark. It seemed tattooed into my skin, but was now completely painless.

What the hell is she doing out of the panic room?

I stormed out of the bathroom, grabbed my robe on the fly, and rushed down the stairs. Heart pounding, I wondered what madness had driven her to leave the panic room.

"Don't freak out!" Laura cried out from the kitchen, hearing my loud steps on the stairs. "You're not dangerous or contagious!"

Those words stopped me dead in my tracks, the tongue lashing I'd been ready to give her evaporating from my mind.

"What?" I asked, as I stepped into the kitchen and stared at her, confused and worried.

She stood before me in a knee-length, black, cotton nightgown with a cute chimp illustration saying 'monkey see, monkey do' and her palms raised in front of her in a surrendering gesture.

Laura took the pan off the stove before turning back to me.

"I did research throughout the night, poked a few close buddies; those hacker friends I've told you about," Laura said, eyeing me cautiously.

"You mean those freak conspiracy theorists?" I asked, disbelieving.

Laura's face heated, and she looked somewhat embarrassed but didn't back down.

"Some of their theories are out there," she conceded, "but while their interpretations are fucked up, the facts behind them are solid."

"How do you know? How can you be so sure as to put your life at risk?" I asked, still reeling.

"Because I *know* them!" she said, giving me an irritated look. "Even though I act irresponsible from time to time, I'm not suicidal. I trust them. Anyway, you're not in psycho mode right now so we can verify if their information was right. If they're wrong, I'll just haul my ass back downstairs."

"Verify how?" I asked, crossing my arms over my chest, trying not to give in to hope too soon.

"They said a simple touch may not do anything, but if part of the Mistwalker enters a person's body, within 24 hours, some symbolic tattoo will appear on their chest," she said with a shrug.

My hand flew to my chest, and I clutched at my heart where a tattoo had indeed appeared.

"Oh my God! You already got yours, didn't you?" Laura asked, her eyes all but popping out of her head.

I nodded slowly and parted my robe to display the tattoo. It looked like an inverted half-moon with a straight bar in the middle, reminiscent of the É letter in the Cyrillic alphabet, but heavily stylized. Pitch black, it stood out against my pale complexion. Staring intently at it gave the impression it wavered.

"What does it do?" I asked in a whisper, transfixed by it, now that my initial panic had faded.

"Richard said it's like a stamp of ownership," she said, with a sympathetic tone. My eyes snapped up to hers, but she, too, was staring at my tattoo, looking fascinated. "Each Mistwalker has his own symbol. It tells the others to fuck off and serves as a beacon to find you."

"Why didn't you text me that?" I asked, fighting the nauseous feeling in my stomach.

"I did! You didn't answer," she said on the defensive. Laura turned to the cupboard and grabbed a pair of plates for us. Looking at me over her shoulder, she continued, "It's not surprising considering the other tidbit of information Richard gave me."

"And what would that be?" I asked, walking up to the table and pulling out a chair.

"That the claimed human ends up getting some pretty hot and steamy wet dreams for the duration of the Mist."

My cheeks burned, all but bursting into flames. Having her suspicions confirmed by my treacherously pale complexion, Laura gaped at me the way one does when witnessing or hearing a particularly juicy bit of gossip.

"You naughty, naughty girl!" she exclaimed.

"You know I'm a deep sleeper," I countered, squirming on my chair.

"True enough," Laura said, giving me an amused look. "You could sleep right through Armageddon."

Too true. My alarm could blare for hours, and I wouldn't hear it. Lucky for me, my internal clock never failed to wake me on time.

"So what does he want? What happens to the human?" I asked, while Laura served our breakfast.

"According to the 'victims' he's spoken to, Richard says the Mistwalker just wants a life mate. That is, the ones that give you that tattoo. Not all of them are good guys, but the ones who brand you aren't evil."

Relief flooded through me. I hadn't gotten the sense he sought to harm me, but still, hearing it from a source that had nailed two of my 'symptoms' reassured me.

"He will give you a choice to go with him or not."

"As in go into the Mist with him?" I asked, flabbergasted.

"Yep. Apparently, he would take you to a safe place where you could live happily ever after and make little Mist babies," she said.

"That's not funny," I said, frowning at her.

"Relax," Laura said while pouring some coffee for me, then for herself. "This is all around good news, in my opinion. You have a choice, and you're not turning into some monster."

"Thank you," I said absentmindedly. After adding two spoons of sugar and some milk, I slowly stirred my cup. "Okay, you're right, but what if I say no?"

Laura shrugged before tucking into her food. "Richard said the girl he spoke to refused to go, and the Mistwalker respected her choice. She was, however, willing to continue the steamy encounters during the Mist, which they have. But others have declined any further contact of any type, and their Mistwalkers have left them alone."

"Just like that?" I asked in a dubious tone.

Laura shrugged again. "That's all I got. Either way, you're not turning into a freak show, and I don't have to spend the next

48 hours in the basement. Like I said, all around good news! Now, I need deets! How's demon sex?"

I nearly choked on the sip of coffee I'd taken. Laura laughed while I glared at her.

"Just eat your food," I said, trying to chase away the memory of that frighteningly pleasurable interlude.

The next 48 hours flew by. Throughout the day, the Mistwalker would touch me with his ghostly presence. He didn't speak or linger, content to give me a drive-by mental caress as if to remind me of his existence or to check that our bond remained. At night, though, he would whisk me away to his realm to launch another sensual assault on me. Like the first time, I would awaken from sleep to find myself surrounded by the Mist, his ethereal hands and mouth unleashing the most delicious torment on my willing body. To my shame, I didn't try to fight but even anticipated it.

After more than three years of celibacy, I was hungry for a release that didn't come from my own hand, and that Mistwalker knew exactly where and how to touch me, giving me the most mind-blowing orgasms I had ever experienced. After Patrick, I'd taken a hiatus on men. I had believed him to be the one. We'd been talking marriage and had just gotten engaged when his ex-girlfriend returned from her four years of studying abroad and expressed the desire to rekindle their relationship. To be fair, Patrick tried to resist and was upfront with me about his warring emotions. It didn't make it any less heartbreaking when he broke off our engagement and returned to her.

Still, I wanted to believe that being horny wasn't my only reason to surrender so easily to a mythical creature. It didn't make sense, yet he felt familiar, safe even. As irrational as it may sound, I didn't doubt for a second that he would stop should I ever ask him to... and meant it. In the three days of the Mist, he never took for himself but focused on my pleasure. He didn't speak or answer any of my questions except with cryptic one-liners that left me as clueless or confused as before.

I didn't even know his name.

But his strength had grown tremendously. He sizzled with it, and the void space he'd been taking me to had begun taking shape with a sky, grass, and the shimmering outline of a mansion. I assumed he intended for us to live there should I accept his offer to join him, but I wouldn't. My place was on Earth, with my sister, my simple life and job as a character artist in video games.

As his expert tongue yet again sent me over the edge, I fleetingly thought that keeping him as a virtual lover, a few days a month, no strings attached, might not be such a bad idea after all. He didn't interact with my physical body, no risk of pregnancy or STDs, and earth-shattering orgasms by the dozen.

Yep. Not a bad deal at all.

Wondrously sated, my Mist-world body humming with pleasurable tremors, I fell back into my real-world body and then contentedly into a peaceful dream. As usual, I'd slept through the City Defense Alarm and had to get confirmation from the news channel that the Mist had indeed lifted. Going around the house, I opened the shutters and the windows to let in some fresh air and daylight.

Although it was Wednesday morning, no one would be expected back to work before Thursday. Since the advent of the Mist, the day before it started and the one after it ended had been declared official holidays, fully compensated by employers. It allowed people who needed long commutes to reach their safe house or shelter to make it on time before the 6:00 PM curfew. At the end of the Mist, the city alarm would only resound two hours later to make sure all the tears in the Veil had closed and any straggling Mistbeasts had perished.

With a heavy heart, I helped my sister pack, and drove her to the train station so she'd be back on campus in time for her classes in the morning. I was grateful we'd been able to spend those three days together after all. Despite her faults—which were actually few—I loved Laura to pieces and missed having her around.

She'd further poked her hacker buddy Richard for any additional information. He'd had none but reiterated that we didn't need to fear for my safety. In the end, that was all that mattered.

Like everyone else, I needed to restock on fresh produce. But grocery stores and pharmacies usually overflowed with customers on the day after the Mist. Even restaurants and bars received heavy traffic from people going crazy after being cooped up in their houses for so many days.

With the weekend right around the corner, I decided to hold off until after work on Friday. I'd stop by Muse Food, the mega supermarket in the heart of the artistic district, a stone's throw away from the studio. Surrounded by museums, exposition halls, and art academies, the market sought to cater to the exotic needs of foreign artists and the exchange students who gravitated to the area.

I mostly cooked on weekends, and I'd been itching for some Moroccan food for a while. On the menu: couscous royal and a tajine kefta. The price of the meat would put a dent in my budget. But after the past few days, I deserved some pampering.

A pretty brunette greeted customers at the entrance to the massive supermarket. Dressed in white with a black artist apron, she picked paintbrush-shaped lollipops which she handed out to customers, pointing out that they came in various flavors and could be found on sale in aisle four. I loved the damn things. They had a creamy, toffee taste to them that demanded seconds. Naturally, I avoided buying them but never snubbed a freebie.

I had a healthy appetite and a healthy weight, although my ideal weight would require shedding an extra ten to fifteen pounds. It didn't trouble me. I was pleased with my appearance but had to be careful in my indulgences and exercise regularly to maintain my figure. Thankfully, aside from ice cream—especially in the form of profiteroles—strawberry shortcakes, and the occasional paintbrush lollipop, I didn't have much of a sweet tooth. Well, okay, add most fruits dipped in chocolate. But who could resist that?

Lips slightly parted, I twirled the lollipop on my tongue while eyeing the contents of my shopping cart, battling the nagging feeling I had forgotten something. I never wrote a shopping list and systematically kicked myself for it.

"Excuse me," a husky male voice said, suavely.

My head jerked to the left and up to look at the towering, muscular, breathtaking man who had spoken. Pitch black hair down to his shoulders, foggy-grey eyes, and chiseled cheekbones that gave his stunning face an air of nobility, but my gaze remained locked on the most perfect lips, which begged to be kissed. They stretched in an amused smile and his soft chuckle snapped me out of my brain tilt. My face heated when I realized I was staring at him, mouth gaping with my lollipop sitting still on my tongue. I yanked it out and closed my mouth with an audible sound.

"Err, hi! Sorry. You took me by surprise. I was lost in thought."

Oh God, now I'm babbling.

My cheeks heated up a notch, and his smile broadened. I cleared my throat.

"Can I help you, sir?" I asked, feeling awkward with my lollipop clutched in my hand.

"I'm new in the neighborhood, and this place is massive," he said with a sheepish look. "Any idea where I could find shortening?"

"Shortening?" I asked, unable to stop myself from scrunching my face in disapproval. "As in to make a pie crust?"

"Yes?" he said, taken aback by my negative response. "You do not approve?"

"I used to," I conceded, "but after a short stay in Paris, it's butter for me, all the way."

He raised an amused eyebrow. "Is that so?"

"Mmhmm," I said with a nod. "But if you *really* want that weird fat instead, I can show you where it's located."

"Weird fat, huh?" His storm-colored eyes sparkled with mirth, giving me all kinds of delicious tingles. "I guess giving butter a try won't hurt. Same amount?"

"Yep!" I said, leaning on my shopping cart.

"All right, then. What about baking powder?"

"Same place as the shortening," I deadpanned.

He blinked, and it was my turn to chuckle.

"Aisle twenty-three, past the frozen products, next to the chips and sweets aisle. Not on the flour shelves but near the sprinkles and other cake decorating stuff. It's a little tricky to find because they usually have some kind of display with free samples creating dead-ends in that area."

"I see," he said slowly, crestfallen.

I laughed again, having deliberately made it sound worse than it was to have an excuse to stick around him a bit longer. Such an odd behavior for me. I wasn't prudish, and definitely not a wallflower, but I also didn't pursue men. The old school part of me still expected the man to make the first move, although I didn't shy away from a little flirting. It had been ages since I'd last acted so boldly… and I freaking loved it!

"This way, newbie," I said, gesturing with my head for him to follow.

He laughed and trailed after me.

"Thank you, Ms…?"

"Jade," I said, flicking my ginger hair over my shoulder while pushing my cart ahead.

"Like your eyes," he said, with a seductive smile.

My stomach swirled with the most exquisite feeling as I forced my face to display a mildly flattered expression instead of fanning myself over him.

"Spot on," I said casually, as we turned into the frozen food aisle.

I couldn't help walking a little taller when I noticed the envious gazes other female shoppers cast my way. He wasn't mine, but for the next few minutes, I got to be the lucky bitch other women wished they could be.

"While newbie is indeed accurate in my case, the name is actually Kazan," he said, smiling.

"So what brings you to our lovely neck of...?" I stopped dead in my tracks and turned to stare at him, my eyes feeling like they'd pop out of my head any minute. "Kazan? As in Kazan Dale, the painter?"

He gave me a cautious look. "Maybe?"

"Oh God! I called Kazan Dale a newbie."

Turning away from him, I closed my eyes, mortified, and held on to my cart with both hands—the lollipop in the right one making it awkward.

Kazan laughed. "Appropriately so," he said gently. "I can't even find my way around a grocery store."

I cracked my lids open and eyed him from the side. He pinched his sexy lips to keep from laughing again.

"Please tell me you're coming out of your retirement, hiatus, or whatever made you stop?" I asked, timidly.

He sobered and gave me a calculating look. "For now, yes."

I perked up. "That's awesome news! I don't mean to go all fangirl on you, but I've been a great admirer of your work since your first posts on the art forums. Please tell me you're planning an exhibition here in the not too distant future?"

"Maybe?"

"You totally are!" I said, fighting the urge to squeal like a schoolgirl. "Note to self, when Kazan Dale says maybe, it means yes."

He laughed again and said, "Maybe."

Putting his hand on the small of my back, he applied a light pressure to encourage me to move on. I realized I'd stopped smack in the middle of the aisle. Although wide, it totally inconvenienced the other patrons.

"I take it you're an artist, too?" he asked.

Blood rushed to my cheeks, with both embarrassment and pleasure that he'd show interest in me.

"Not of your caliber, but I'm pretty decent," I said, trying to sound the right level of modest. "I'm a character artist and the art lead of my project. Video games," I added as he opened his mouth to ask a question.

His brow shot up, not with the elitist disdain I'd expected, but with genuine, delighted surprise. My liking of—instant infatuation with—him went up another notch.

"I love video games," he said, with sincere enthusiasm. "3D modeling?"

"Yes, although I do a lot of concept art on my tablet and still paint in my small studio at home."

"I would love to see your work," Kazan said as we stopped in front of the shelves containing baking powder.

"I... Wow, I'd be honored for you to look at it," I said, blown away. "Here, let me give you my business card. You'll find the link to my online portfolio on it."

I rummaged through my purse and pulled out a card, which I extended to him. He took it with his left hand then leaned forward to pick up the baking powder on the shelf next to me with the other hand. His chest brushed against my back, making me weak in the knees. My breath caught in my throat as he straightened and our eyes met. I remained transfixed by his grey eyes, which darkened, the heady scent of his subtle cologne making me dizzy. Mesmerized, I drowned in the foggy depths of his gaze as time seemed to slow.

A sharp pain in my chest snapped me out of my daze. My hand flew to my Mist tattoo, which suddenly flared up, burning cold, with a tugging sensation as if energy were being sucked out of me.

Kazan flinched and blood drained from his face. He blinked and staggered a couple of steps away from me. He cast a worried look towards me, appearing to become worn out at an alarming rate.

Oh God! The Mistwalker is leeching him! Leeching us!

I could feel my own energy draining away quickly and moved away from Kazan as well.

"Well, thank you for your help," Kazan said, suddenly eager to leave. "I think I'm more jetlagged than I realized. I better head back, but I'll check it out," he added, waving my card.

"Take care," I said, my chest tightening with an irrational sense of loss. "It was a pleasure meeting you."

"Likewise," Kazan said.

With a final smile and head nod, he walked away.

The pulling sensation and freezing burn faded away as suddenly as they had begun, and with them, the Mistwalker's presence.

CHAPTER 3
JADE

Over the next three days, I fell into something of a depression. The Mistwalker had not manifested himself again after that major cock-blocking. However, neither had Kazan. The number of views on my portfolio had increased, but that didn't mean they came from him.

My obsession with both of them felt unhealthy. The Mistwalker couldn't be helped. Everything about him and his agenda remained a mystery. Based on that incident in the supermarket, he could literally be trying to mess up my life. For the first time in three years, I'd finally met someone who stirred emotions that had been buried deep since Patrick left, and he messed it up.

My fascination with Kazan had started six years ago, the very first time I'd seen one of his paintings. As a huge Luis Royo fan, I'd been rendered speechless by Kazan's art, similar in theme but so photo-realistic I'd initially thought they'd been photo manipulations before realizing they were 100% hand painted.

He'd wink in and out of existence, sometimes posting new work and doing exhibitions over long stretches then falling off the face of the Earth for months. A little over three years ago, his agent had declared that Kazan would be taking an extended leave from both public life—which had mostly been non-existent to begin with—and from painting—with no real explanation or justification. It broke my heart, and I'd cussed the heck out of the media and tabloids who I held responsible for constantly hounding him.

Kazan never wanted his picture taken, apparently so that he could maintain a normal life outside of his art. He'd had no known relationship or significant other. Rumors had it he was gay and kept it under wraps for fear it might negatively impact his career. That never made much sense to me as artistic circles had tons of gays and lesbians. In truth, it seemed to me it would have made him even more welcome in the inner circles.

Yet, from my brief encounter with Kazan, I didn't get the sense of him being socially inept; quite the opposite. Despite his soft and gentle demeanor, he'd possessed an undeniable strength —predatory energy even—which lurked beneath his gorgeous exterior. I tingled all over again just thinking about him.

Looking at my sketchbook, I sighed at yet another drawing of Kazan. In the first four days of the past week, nearly twenty pages had been dedicated to the Mistwalker. The last three days, Kazan had dominated. Some of the pictures should go straight to the garbage; not because they were bad, but because I'd taken some very naughty liberties. If Laura saw this—and she always browsed through my sketchbooks—I'd never hear the end of it. This latest portrait, though, I actually wanted to paint.

I eyed the blank canvas sitting on my easel and chewed my bottom lip. As I rose to step towards it, my phone chimed, indicating a new text message. I cast an absent-minded look at it, my mind already on the painting, then did a double take.

'Hi Jade. It's Kazan. Loved your portfolio!'

My heart skipped a beat. I plopped myself back into my desk chair and grabbed my phone with greedy hands.

'Wow! Thanks! Can't believe you checked it out.'

'Of course, I did. Can I call you? Is it a good time?'

Could he call me? Seriously? I'd hoped he'd do exactly that when I gave him my business card. Not hearing from him for the first 24 hours had been normal; it would have made him look too eager, although that hadn't stopped me from wishing. Waiting 48 hours had sucked. By the third day, today, I'd started wallowing in self-pity.

'Sure. Not busy right now.'

The phone rang moments later. I counted two seconds before answering to avoid revealing how much I'd been dying to hear his sultry voice again.

"Hello," I said.

"Hello, pretty lady," Kazan answered, his suave, bedroom voice making my insides liquefy. "Why would you doubt I'd look at your work? I said I would, and my word is important to me."

I squirmed with both pleasure and embarrassment at his gently chastising tone. "I didn't mean to doubt you, but you must get a million groupies asking you to check their work, so I figured you wouldn't get around to mine in the near future."

He chuckled, sending a delicious shiver down my spine.

"I don't have groupies," he said, sounding amused. "They've all moved on to new pastures after my last disappearing act, giving me plenty of time to examine the beautiful work of a long-time admirer who doesn't fangirl on me."

It was my turn to laugh at having my own words used on me.

"Well, that long-time admirer is flattered," I said, a smile in my voice.

"I especially liked the fierce, green-eyed, red-headed dragon slayer and her fearless, freckled sidekick."

"Oh God! I can't believe I left that up!" I said, my face burning with embarrassment. "It's an old drawing that my little sister Laura dared me to make of us as dragon slayers in the kind of ridiculous, barely-there armor that women in fantasy art and video games usually wear."

"You mean the type of outfit women in my paintings wear?"

Ugh... Can I put my foot in my mouth any deeper?

"Well, your art is different," I answered lamely.

"Really? How?"

I squirmed on my chair, not quite knowing how to answer. As much as I hated the objectification of women in games, Kazan's sexy, semi-erotic art didn't offend me in the least. I found it beautiful.

"Honestly, I can't give a rational answer," I confessed. "I think it bothers me in games because it's all about titillating young boys and reduces female characters to pure eye candy. In your paintings, it feels like you're celebrating the beauty of a woman's body, her great inner-strength wrapped in a deceptive fragility. When I look at the women in your paintings, I want to be them."

"Even the ones in the arms of monsters?"

His voice had dropped an octave, making my skin erupt in goosebumps.

"Especially those," I said, softly.

And that was true. I'd always felt a little twisted about my love for monster and alien romance novels and the far too scarce movies in the genre. I'd seen every possible version of Beauty and the Beast and never missed a single sci-fi movie involving some hot alien falling for a human female... or vice-versa. Although I preferred the former as it was easier to picture myself as the lucky lady.

The silence stretched for a couple of seconds. I held my breath, waiting for his response to my overly honest admission.

"I want to paint you, Jade. Will you let me?" he said at last.

My stomach lurched, and my heart leapt.

"What?" I whispered, refusing to believe my ears.

"I want to paint you. Will you model for me?"

Are you fucking kidding me? HELL YES!

"Err… I've never posed professionally."

"I don't care. You're perfect. That's all I could think about from the first time I laid eyes on you. Please say yes."

"O… Okay," I breathed out, still disbelieving he had truly asked me, and even more that I had accepted.

"Wonderful! Can we start this Saturday?" Kazan asked.

The genuine happiness in his voice made me tingle again. That man had the most incredible effect on me.

I felt my eyes bulge. "So soon?"

"I have decided to hold a painting exhibition right after the next Mist," Kazan said. "I want your painting to be part of it. Which means we have to sign a standard modeling contract."

Wait. What?!

"Ugh… I don't know about that…"

"Think about it," he said, quickly. "You don't have to commit to anything right now. Either way, I want to paint you. That gives you almost a month to reflect on whether you want to be part of the exhibit. If you don't agree in the end, then I'll at least have it as part of my personal collection."

"All right," I said, overwhelmed by conflicting emotions.

I had a respectably nice body. Although a bit more plump than his usual models, Kazan would definitely make me look drop dead gorgeous. I wanted to see myself through his eyes and I especially wanted to see which monster, if any, he'd pair me with. But, even dressed, the highly suggestive poses and outfits of the women in his paintings left little to the imagination. I didn't feel comfortable with the public—and likely my coworkers—seeing me like that. Then again, to be Kazan Dale's muse, if only for a single painting, held some serious bragging rights.

"Thank you, Jade," Kazan said, his voice like a caress. "We should celebrate! How about dinner and a movie on Friday evening? I've heard good things about that new superhero movie..."

Oh God! Is he asking me out on a date?

"Mutant Uprising?" I asked, trying to sound casual about it despite my urge to squeal. "I'd love to! I'd actually planned on going to see it this weekend."

"Awesome! Any food preferences?"

"Surprise me," I said. "I eat anything, except insects and food that's still moving on my plate." He chuckled, making me smile. "Fancy and stuck up places aren't my cup of tea either."

"Noted. I'll call you tomorrow with the exact time and place. Does that work for you?"

"Sounds good."

"All right. Have a good evening, Jade. I'll talk to you soon."

"Good night, Kazan."

After he hung up, I stared disbelieving at my phone for a few moments, then screamed like the fangirl I denied being. All thoughts of painting forgotten, I raced to my bedroom to start looking for the perfect outfit to wear on our date; casual with some understated chic flair.

As promised, he called me the day after to confirm our plans. Normally, I would have been at my Zumba fitness class like every Wednesday, but I might have missed his call had I been in the middle of dancing. Then I suffered through the endless wait until Friday evening.

Wanting to surprise me—as per my request—he came to pick me up in a cab. He texted me as they pulled up to the house. I stepped out to find him standing by the vehicle, looking ridiculously sexy in a pair of black, slim biker jeans, an artfully distressed, black shirt, and heavy, black boots. His hair pulled back in a tail, revealed the silver rings in each of his pierced ears and the perfect bone structure of his stunning face.

My asymmetrical little black dress and medium heeled black sandals seemed the perfect match to his rebel outfit.

"You look stunning," he said, while holding the door for me.

Not sure how to greet him, I was relieved when he placed a hand on my hip and leaned forward to kiss my cheek.

"You don't look too shabby yourself, Mr. Dale," I said while entering the car and scooting over to make room for him.

"Why thank you, Ms. Eastwood," Kazan said while taking a seat next to me.

For a second, I wondered how the heck he knew my last name, then remembered that it was written on my business card.

Kazan signaled for the driver to go. As he didn't give him the name or address of our destination, I assumed he'd already done so before I arrived. We made casual conversation during the twenty minute drive downtown. He smelled and looked good enough to eat. Lucky for him, we pulled up in front of the Golden Wings, barbecue and grill, before I could lose control and jump him.

"Is this where we're going?" I asked, pointing at the winged sign of the restaurant after he finished settling with the driver.

"Yes," he said with a cautious look in his eyes. "I hope that's not a problem?"

"Are you kidding me? I looooove Golden Wings!" I said, grinning from ear to ear. "I'm a sucker for ribs and chicken wings, and they make the best ones for miles around!"

Kazan beamed at me. "Then let's not delay any further and get you some barbecue."

He took my hand so naturally I didn't resist as he led me into the restaurant. While it attracted a casually-chic clientele, it didn't cater to poor patrons. With the steep price of meat, I only came here once or twice a year, usually for special occasions. The wooden décor, muted lighting, and padded booths made for the ideal romantic dinner.

A pretty brunette came to take our order. Her eyes lingered on Kazan who paid her no attention, his entire focus on me. He was scoring brownie points with me by the shovel full. At my request, we started off with a giant onion bloom.

"Anything to drink?" the waitress asked.

"Sangria for me, please."

She nodded and turned to Kazan whose gaze seemed to go blank for a second.

"I'll have the same," he said, after a beat.

She left to fetch our drinks while we browsed the menu.

"What will you have?" I asked.

"I believe someone said ribs and chicken wings," Kazan said with a smile.

"I can't have both," I said. "It's too much food."

Not to mention too steep a price.

"Exactly. So, pick the one you crave the most, and I'll get the other one so you can take some from me, too," he said, matter-of-fact.

"Oh wow, you don't have to do that!" I said, touched none-theless. "You should pick something you like."

"I also enjoy ribs and chicken wings, so either choice is no hardship for me."

"Are you sure?" I asked, still feeling bad.

"I wouldn't offer otherwise," he said with a gentle smile. "Go ahead, choose!"

I ended up picking the ribs, the wings making it easier to steal a couple from him. As expected, the meal proved to be beyond finger-licking good. While Kazan did eat, I couldn't help noticing that he barely drank his Sangria and didn't clean his plate. For such a tall and muscular man, I'd expected him to put away gargantuan portions.

Before I could ask him if he didn't like the food, the waitress dropped by to ask if we wanted coffee or dessert. Normally, I would have been all over the chocolate mousse cake, but I needed to save room for popcorn. Kazan settled the bill and held my hand again as we exited the restaurant. I loved the casual possessiveness of it all and how natural it felt.

We strolled through the brightly lit streets in the pleasantly warm, late April evening. Friday nights in the normally quiet and quaint Cordell City always buzzed with activity. Despite its turn-of-the-century Victorian charm, it offered all the modern amenities one could wish for. Becoming a North-American mecca for traditional arts, and increasingly, digital arts, had successfully attracted a young and hip population which sauntered past us seeking their own entertainment.

With forty-five minutes to kill before the show, we took our time walking to the movie theatre, browsing store windows, and admiring street performers. One particularly skilled illusionist drew quite the crowd, forcing me to stand even closer to Kazan who wrapped his arm around my waist. I leaned against him, and he tightened his hold. Feeling emboldened, I slipped my own arm around him and pressed myself further against his muscular side.

Not wanting to be late, we eventually headed for the theater, his arm resting on my shoulders and mine still wrapped around him. This felt like high school when neither party wanted to spell out how they felt but were seriously crushing over each other and tentatively touching each other to see if their love interest would balk.

A few meters from the theater, the throbbing in my chest manifested itself again. The burning sensation increasing at an alarming rate. I could almost feel the presence of the Mistwalker at the back of my head. Oblivious to my discomfort, Kazan released me with obvious reluctance to go validate the tickets he had reserved online.

Please don't fuck this up for me. Let me enjoy this evening.

I felt like I'd just jumped headfirst into crazy town trying to speak to the Mistwalker in my mind, but what other option did I have? The perfect man—at least for now—had just walked into my life, and our attraction appeared to be mutual. My stomach knotted with apprehension that this evening would be ruined.

The pain receded almost as soon as Kazan let go of me. I couldn't say if the Mistwalker had taken pity on me in response to my plea or was no longer punishing me for allowing another male to touch *his* Jade. Kazan returned with the tickets, and we walked hand in hand to the concession stands.

Knowing I wanted popcorn, Kazan grabbed the large bag and two drinks combo, although he exchanged his soda for a bottle of mineral water. When the stand worker asked with or without butter, I immediately said 'with' and stared at Kazan with pleading eyes.

He laughed. "The lady has spoken," Kazan said to the stand worker.

She nodded and gave him a discreet once over. In her late teens, she'd be prettier without such thick layers of makeup. My skin itched just looking at her.

We settled down in the center of the theater, the lights fading moments later. To my relief, while the Mistwalker's presence remained constant throughout the movie, like a tingling sensation at my nape, and a dull throb around his tattoo on my chest, it didn't interfere with my enjoyment of the evening. You'd almost think he was watching the movie with us.

To my disappointment, Kazan didn't try to get frisky with me despite the darkness surrounding us. While I ate the popcorn—since he only took a handful where there hadn't been any butter—his arm rested on my shoulder, his thumb caressing my upper arm. We didn't speak. Even though I wanted to keep chatting with him, I hated people that babbled during movies and was grateful for his silence as well. We left with half the bag of popcorn still full but his water bottle fully drained.

Aside from his drink, the movie, the illusionist and, of course, my delightful company, I suspected Kazan hadn't much enjoyed the rest of the evening. He'd clearly tried to please me with the wings and the butter on the popcorn, while not liking them himself. As for the Sangria, that, too, he'd barely touched. But it was the blank look—although the word 'panicked' kept popping into my mind—that had struck me when the waitress asked him what he wanted.

If we ever went on another date—and God knows I wanted to—I'd make sure he ordered things he liked. I couldn't risk him getting turned off from spending time with me because he was constantly forcing himself to do things he didn't want to.

After walking for ten minutes without catching a single free cab, the rare ones we saw getting snagged right from under us by others, we decided to walk three blocks down, away from Main Street, where we'd more likely find a taxi stand. Wrapping his arm around me, Kazan tucked me under his arm as we padded slowly down the blissfully peaceful sidewalk.

We talked at length, and Kazan inquired about my past. His obvious interest in me and my life touched me deeply. My teenage years had been tough. So, I did my best not to become a Debbie Downer as I gave him an overview of that time.

"Our parents died in a dumb car accident when I was twelve," I said, glad that after so many years, I could finally speak of it without choking up. "It's been just Laura and me ever since, being passed around from one uncle or aunt to the next. Despite the circumstances, the first couple of years had been great with our grandmother. But after her stroke, our parents' siblings had to carry the torch. They did their best, but we were an extra burden they weren't prepared to handle."

"I'm sorry," Kazan said, commiserating.

"It's okay. In many ways, we'd been luckier than many other kids in our situation who ended up wards of the State or landed in foster homes and got separated. Laura is a pain in the rear sometimes, but I wouldn't trade her for all the gold in the world. Do you have siblings?"

"Not really," he said as we crossed the deserted street.

"Not really?" I asked, lifting my head to give him a confused look.

"I was an orphan, too, left alone almost immediately after my birth." He shrugged. "I grew up a loner, mostly by choice, then spread my wings as soon as I could. It wasn't miserable, just lonely at times, which explains why I'm so socially awkward."

"You're not socially awkward at all!" I exclaimed.

"Not with you. For some reason, you instantly made me feel at ease, like I've known you forever."

And I had felt the same about him. I opened my mouth to tell him as much when the sound of footsteps behind us drew my attention. Looking over his shoulder, the hooded silhouettes of two men walking towards us made my heart lurch. Kazan looked over his shoulder as well and glanced at them before facing ahead, apparently dismissive of their presence. Although we picked up the pace slightly, we didn't move half as fast as I would have liked us to.

Despite his nonchalant expression, I felt Kazan's rippling muscles tense against me. I couldn't say if my nerves were playing tricks on me or if the two men's brisk steps had in fact accelerated. Reaching the next intersection, we crossed the street to the opposite sidewalk, hoping they would keep walking straight ahead. My heart sank when they continued to shadow us, closing the distance between us.

The throbbing in my chest grew exponentially as my tattoo flared. The tingling I'd come to associate with the presence of the Mistwalker became so strong, I all but expected to see him appear before me.

For once, I would genuinely have welcomed him.

As soon as we reached the other sidewalk, Kazan shoved me towards the building ahead of us and turned around to face our stalkers. Stumbling forward, I raised my hands in front of me to keep my balance. My breath caught in my throat as I turned and saw one of our would-be muggers had pulled out a knife. While preferable to a gun, it could still seriously hurt Kazan. I didn't know what to do. Self-defense classes said to scream, throw my purse or wallet in one direction and run in the other, but my gut told me Kazan wouldn't run.

The look in his eyes spelled death.

"For your own sake," Kazan said, his voice chillingly calm and threatening, "turn around and walk away. Or I promise a most unpleasant outcome for you."

The man on the left, whose features I couldn't see, shaded as they were by his hoodie, chuckled at Kazan's threat.

"You've got big balls, big man," he said, taunting Kazan, "but you might not be so cocky once I start messing up your woman's pretty face with my blade. Hand over your wallet, that fancy watch, and your jewelry, and you get to go home and fuck her sweet pussy. Challenge us, and maybe we'll fuck her raw after we're done spending your money."

I was okay with that first suggestion. A few dollars, even a couple of hundred, weren't worth either of our lives.

"Come and get them."

No! Kazan, no!

Just as the thought crossed my mind, my vision blurred, and a dark mist took form between Kazan and me before wrapping itself around him. Neither Kazan nor his attackers appeared to see it. The leader of the two thugs took a couple of steps towards Kazan who burst into action. Moving at inhuman speed, he smashed his fist into the thief's face with a sickening, wet sound. Blood exploding from his face, teeth falling out of his mouth, the thug flopped to the ground, unconscious or dead, without emitting a single sound.

"You son of a whore!" the second thief yelled, throwing himself at Kazan with his own blade raised.

He slashed frantically at Kazan who dodge with impossible speed and ease, like a twisted game of cat and mouse, quickly tiring his aggressor. In an unexpected move, Kazan ducked, spun out of the blade's trajectory and, using the momentum of his rotation, slammed his fist into the hooded man's side. Even from where I stood, I heard his ribs cracking. Covering my mouth with both hands, I silenced the horrified scream that wanted to tear out of my throat.

The wounded man doubled over in pain, his scream snuffed out seconds later by Kazan bringing down his fist at the back of his head. He collapsed, unconscious, a couple of meters away from his partner.

Despite the terror making me tremble from head to toe, relief flooded me to see the two men still breathing. Although they'd brought this on themselves, and as much as Kazan currently frightened me, I didn't want him charged with manslaughter, even if in self-defense. No judge would ever believe he'd damaged these men this severely with his mere fists.

"Do not be afraid, my Jade. No one will ever harm you."

I squealed at the Mistwalker's voice in my head. Kazan turned abruptly towards me at the sound, as if looking for the source of the threat. He blinked and appeared dazed for a moment as the dark mist around him faded into oblivion. The tingling sensation at my nape and the throbbing on my chest disappeared.

The Mistwalker was gone.

The feral look on Kazan face melted, replaced by worry as he moved towards me. On instinct, I stepped backwards until the brick wall of the building behind me pressed against my back.

The hurt expression in Kazan's eyes clawed at my heart. Had he felt the Mistwalker taking him over, or lending him his power, or whatever that had been?

"It's okay," Kazan said in a soft voice. He approached me slowly, carefully, as if I were a frightened animal—which, to be honest, wasn't far from the truth. "It's over. You're safe. They can't hurt you now."

Or anyone else, anytime soon…

Except, *they* no longer scared me. *He* did!

"Let's go to that cab stand and get you home."

I didn't resist when he gently took my hand and drew me towards him. Feeling numb, I cast a brief glance over his shoulder at the unconscious men, thankfully still breathing, and let Kazan guide me down the last block to Juniper Street where a handful of taxis awaited customers.

We should call the cops or at least an ambulance.

The thought replayed in my mind, but my mouth refused to open and speak it out loud. Frazzled, I stood in a daze while Kazan opened the cab's door for me. Before I could get in, he cupped my face in his hands.

"You're safe now, Jade. The driver will take you home, and everything will be fine."

Despite the fear he had inspired in me only minutes ago, a wave of panic surged through me at the thought of not having him by my side.

"You're not coming with me?" I asked, gripping his shirt at the waist.

"I have to call the cops and an ambulance for those assholes. Someone needs to handle this."

Right...

Although relieved that the authorities would be informed, that he wasn't just abandoning the scene, I couldn't fully process what was happening. Never had I wanted to be home so badly and for all of this to be over. Kazan leaned forward and brushed his lips against mine. I'd wanted to respond but remained stoic. It didn't appear to upset him.

Our first kiss... wasted.

"Go on, my darling," he said, taking a step back and gesturing with his head for me to enter the vehicle.

I got into the car, and Kazan closed the door for me before walking up to the driver's window. He pulled out a fifty-dollar bill, almost double the cost of the fare, and handed it to the driver.

"Please take her home and wait until she's inside the house before leaving."

The cabbie nodded, and Kazan gave him my address before turning to look at me through the backseat window. He gestured for me to lower it. I complied.

"Call me as soon as you arrive to let me know you're fine, all right?"

"I will."

"Good girl."

He smiled and watched us drive off before turning back to retrace our steps. As the cab u-turned to head back out of City Center, I stared at Kazan, pulling his mobile phone from his pocket to call the cops.

It wasn't until halfway through the trip home that it finally hit me that we could have died tonight. My entire body began to shake, and tears gathered in my eyes. Blinking them back, I hugged myself, wishing for Kazan's arms around me instead.

He should have stayed with me.

Despite feeling abandoned, he'd made the right call by staying. I couldn't have. He no doubt sensed it and sent me away before I fell apart, and yet, I didn't want to be alone. Even the presence of the Mistwalker would have been welcomed. As much as he scared me, I no longer doubted that he wanted me safe.

The trip home took forever. At last, we pulled up to the house. Finding my neighbors, Mr. and Mrs. Palmer, sitting in their matching rocking chairs on their front porch had a soothing effect on me, bringing back a sense of normalcy. As soon as the weather turned warm enough, the older couple never missed a chance to enjoy a nightcap and casual conversations under a night sky. I'd joined them on the odd occasion.

After thanking the driver, I exited the cab, nodded at the

Palmers, and walked up to my front door. Once inside the house, I waved at the cabbie who bowed his head before driving off.

Heading straight for the living room, I all but collapsed on the couch and immediately whipped out my phone to call Kazan. He answered at the first ring.

"You're home," he said in greeting.

"Yes, thank you," I said, oddly comforted by the sound of his voice. "Where are you?" I asked, dreading his response.

"On my way home."

I recoiled slightly in surprise. Kicking off my shoes, I raised my feet onto the couch, hugging my knees to my chest.

"That was fast. Did the cops give you a hard time?"

His slight pause before answering made me nervous.

"I didn't wait for them," he confessed.

My jaw dropped. "What?"

"I didn't want to get the third degree from them or be stuck with all the paperwork. For sure, they would have asked me to file a complaint of some sort," he said somewhat defensively. "I stayed long enough to make sure our attackers were taken care of, then I left."

I nodded to myself. In his shoes, I probably wouldn't have stuck around either, especially considering the serious damage he'd inflicted.

"Okay. I… I'm glad you handled it. I was in a bit of a state of shock."

"I know, my darling. I'm so sorry this happened."

"It's not your fault. Thank you for protecting me."

"Always, Jade. Always."

The solemn way in which he spoke the words sounded like an oath. It moved me deeply.

"I hate that our evening ended this way. Tomorrow, I promise to make it up to you," Kazan said.

My stomach dropped. It finally sank in that, the whole ride home, I'd actually been leaning toward not going to his place to model for him. A part of me wanted to, the other part was screaming pretty loudly that this had been a sign, to end it now before it got even more complicated.

"You *are* still coming, right?" Kazan asked when the silence stretched.

"I... hmmm..."

"Don't do this, Jade," he whispered, his voice hurt and pleading. "I'm sorry things went belly up tonight, but don't let those thugs ruin our plans even more."

His pained tone melted my heart.

"Kazan..."

"Please, say yes. Please!"

I inhaled deeply, knowing myself to be defeated. "Okay."

"Promise!" he insisted, his voice more forceful.

"I promise."

"I will hold you to it, Jade. If you're not here by 9:00 AM, I'll camp on your front yard and make a ruckus until you come out."

"Nine in the morning? On a Saturday?" I exclaimed, wondering if he had lost his ever-loving mind.

"Models are usually expected to show up at 7:00 AM," he deadpanned. "Be grateful for my leniency."

"But..."

"Nine, Jade. Or prepare to explain to your neighbors who the crazy man is outside your house."

"Fine, you bully," I mumbled.

He chuckled. "Sleep well, Jade. I really enjoyed spending time with you tonight and can't wait to see you tomorrow."

My stomach fluttered, and I couldn't help the smile stretching across my face. Damn the man and his ability to soothe me so easily.

"Good night, Kazan."

CHAPTER 4
KAZAN

Seething with rage, I struggled to remain contained in my human vessel. A single, primal desire dominated my thoughts: track and kill those who had threatened my mate. They had not only ruined Jade's peaceful happiness and frightened her, they'd also forced me to show myself and my power to her on the Mortal Plane, before she was ready.

My woman feared me and what I represented. Every minute before the next Mist counted to make her understand that no other being, in this plane or any other world, could make her happier than I could. I was made for her, and she was the only female that could ever touch my heart. This human vessel would serve to make Jade realize she belonged by my side. I needed her to willingly cross the Veil into the Mist Plane.

But those two bastards had almost ruined it all.

The scent of her fear still stung my nose and fueled my anger. Traveling the Mortal Plane without the Mist to sustain me heavily taxed my energy reserves, as did this vessel. Nine years I had waited to make contact with my mate, and it had finally happened, thanks to her sister's carelessness. I'd gorged on the life force of Mistbeasts for the remainder of the Mist to build enough energy reserves to remake this form in order to remain by her side and lure her to me. This one battle with the thugs had all but drained me. Failing to replenish myself soon would force me to cross the Veil, and I wouldn't be able to return to my Jade until the next Mist.

That wouldn't do.

As my human vessel closed the distance to the unconscious thugs, I shifted the fragments of my essence, planted inside of their bodies when I struck them, that prevented them from waking. In spite of their severe wounds, I didn't want to chase them through the streets of the Mortal Plane or risk other humans finding them before I could deal with them. I seized control of their vocal chords instead, as they came to, keeping them from screaming for help.

The revolting scent of their fear and pain filled my nostrils. I hated to feed on negative emotions, or on the life force of the sickly or the evil, but this vermin, I would enjoy devouring. Their terror rose like a tidal wave as I showed myself in my full, ethereal glory and gorged on their emotions. Unable to scream, their pleading eyes looked beyond me at my human vessel. But no help would come for them this night. Hovering over each of them in turn, I drained their life force, leaving just enough for them to remain in a semi-vegetative state. In time, months, if not years, they had a slim chance of recovering. Although killing them would have pleased me more, sucking their life force any further would leave a shriveled husk behind that couldn't be explained in any rational fashion.

But more importantly, it would upset Jade.

My beautiful Jade... Her happiness, the feel of her body against my human vessel, the heady scent of her arousal, and the delectable taste of her essence constituted the most divine nectar. I wanted to drown in it. Soon, she would be completely mine.

The distant sound of sirens prompted me to return to my

human vessel, hurry back to the cab stand, and get away from this place. My Jade would call me any minute, now.

D espite sensing her presence before she'd even entered the building, the chime of the doorbell startled me. I forced myself to walk at a measured pace to the door before opening it. Jade looked breathtaking in a simple, knee-length, beige summer dress with butterfly print around the hem. Until this moment, I'd feared she wouldn't come.

"Five minutes early," I said in greeting, smiling and gesturing for her to come in. "I guess the threat of making a ruckus in your neighborhood worked! I'll have to keep that in mind."

The slight tension stiffening her shoulders lessened as she chuckled.

"You have no idea how stuck up some of them can be. That was a most cruel threat," she said with false displeasure as she shrugged her black shawl off her shoulders.

The weather forecasted another warm and sunny day, but the morning remained a little chilly.

"You look beautiful," I said, taking the shawl from her then leaning in to kiss her.

She tensed again, this time not in fear, but with excitement and anticipation. While our relationship was clearly moving into a romantic one, the previous night's last-minute fiasco had prevented us from concluding it in any kind of formal way. I needed to erase any doubt from her as to where our status stood.

Wrapping my free arm around her waist, I drew her closer to me and brushed my lips against hers. I stopped to look into her eyes. Although this was her chance to pull away, I already knew she wouldn't. Reading her emotions in the Mortal Plane constantly challenged me, but never when it came to her attraction for me or her state of arousal. However, she needed to know that I would move at her pace and not push further than she could handle. Her shy smile in response sufficed for me to go for seconds. This time, I kissed her with conviction, my hand sliding up her back to cup her nape.

When her lips parted, I tilted my head to the side to deepen the kiss. As our tongues made their first acquaintance, I reveled in her naturally sweet taste, further enhanced by the mint she had eaten, probably on her way here. Jade leaned into me, her soft moan—barely a sigh—the most beautiful of sounds. I felt myself harden, a terrible hunger rising from deep within.

Not now. Not yet.

With much reluctance, I ended the kiss, pleased that her disappointment echoed my own.

"Come on, let me give you a tour," I said, taking a step back. Linking our fingers together, I pulled her along with me.

My loft was the one thing which gave me great joy that didn't directly involve Jade. It had taken me years to build enough wealth on the Mortal Plane to acquire it. Located on the twelfth floor of a renovated, former industrial building, it boasted sand-colored hardwood floors, white walls, and exposed beam coffered ceilings. In the absence of neighbors in front, no curtains covered the large French windows. Not a single painting or image decorated my walls, but various sculptures rested against them or sat on a few wooden shelves. Dark wood couches with plush, khaki cushions surrounded a coffee table in the same style and all faced a massive, stone fireplace. The windows of the gourmet kitchen gave a breathtaking view of the bay.

The awed look on Jade's face made me feel warm inside. She absent-mindedly caressed the exposed, light-brown bricks of the left wall with her fingertips, her gaze lingering on the door past the breakfast nook. She glanced around the loft at the other three doors at the back of the living room.

Eager to show her my studio, I led her by the hand to the

room past the kitchen. Jade's eyes widened, and her lips parted in awe as we stepped inside. She took a few steps towards the left corner of the room where a work table and multiple shelves displayed a vast array of painting paraphernalia, from pencils to brushes, acrylics to oils, watercolors to inks, and everything else in between. Her eyes lingered on a stack of sketchbooks.

"They're empty," I said, guessing the reason behind the sudden spark of curiosity in her eyes.

She pursed her lips in the most adorable pout and looked to the right corner of the room where I kept stacks of canvases of various sizes, some bought pre-made; the canvas boards I had created myself, placed on a separate pile. Her gaze roamed past them to a series of sketches stuck on the wall before trailing to the free-standing display panels aligned in four rows of three in front of them. A painting hung on both faces of the panels, but as they stood sideways to us, she stepped forward to have a look at them.

"My Demonica series," I said, suddenly nervous about her reaction. "This is intended as my next exhibition. No one else has seen it, not even my agent."

Jade's sharp intake of breath when she gazed upon the first one told me I had succeeded. She chewed her bottom lip, her eyes drinking in the image of the massive, dark-grey demon with his head thrown back in ecstasy and his groin pressing into the rear of a beautiful, mostly naked human female, her lips parted in the throes of passion. The next painting had the same couple, this time with the woman sitting on a throne of skulls, her legs spread wide, one of them resting over the arm of the throne. With one hand, she fondled her left breast beneath her torn bustier and with the other, she gripped the right horn of the demon who knelt before her, his face buried between her thighs. The third picture, far tamer than the previous two, displayed the fully naked woman asleep, sitting on the demon's lap, cradled in his arm, one of his bat wings partially sheltering her as he gazed lovingly upon her peaceful face.

"Wow," Jade whispered. "This is incredible."

She walked to the other side of the first row of panels to look at the paintings on the back. This second set presented a new couple in three different scenes, always two passionate encounters and one tender moment. With each painting, the scent of Jade's arousal grew steadily, driving me insane with desire. Her reaction when she reached the fifth set with the succubus and human male couple almost undid me. Of all her nightly fantasies —which had inspired every one of these paintings—Jade incarnating a succubus had been among her most intense and frequently recurring dreams. Although in the previous paintings I'd chosen models that didn't resemble her, in this one, I'd deliberately picked a fiery redhead.

My paintings affected her so strongly because they were a physical replica of her deepest and darkest fantasies, the passionate wet dreams that burrowed deep into her subconscious as dreams faded with the morning light.

By the time she finished examining the twenty-fourth and last painting in the series, the scent of her arousal permeated the room. Cheeks flushed, eyes smoldering, her body thrummed with unfulfilled sexual energy. It took all my willpower not to drag her to my bedroom and ravish her. The crushing waves of her need made it all the more difficult. I couldn't read her mind, but her emotions and desires flashed through mine like a collage. Right this instant, she wanted me to lift her up, slam her back against the wall, and fuck her senseless.

How I wanted to…

But while she would give in to it, maybe even welcome it in the moment, it would break things between us, or majorly set us back, once she regained her senses. She wanted to be properly courted and desired for more than the use of her wondrous body.

"I simply have no words. I think this is your best collection yet. You're going to blow them away."

I smiled, my chest bursting with pride. In truth, I didn't give a shit what the public thought beyond the fact that it gave me the means to court her on the Mortal Plane and would allow me to give her the comfortable life she deserved should Jade choose to remain in this realm rather than cross the Veil with me.

"I'm thrilled you like them," I said, cupping her face between my hands, "because I want to add six more pieces featuring you."

"Six?" she asked, her eyes widening in surprise. "But all the other couples are only three."

"You will be the centerpiece," I said before capturing her mouth in a hungry kiss.

Lips parting to welcome my invading tongue, she immediately responded, her delicate hands gripping my waist. Unaware she was even doing it, Jade broadcast flashing images of me ripping the clothes off her back, tossing her down onto the varnished wooden floor, and taking her with savage abandon.

Breaking the kiss that had fanned the inferno raging in my loins, instead of appeasing it, my thumbs gently caressed her cheeks.

"My beautiful Jade," I whispered.

She shuddered, her eyes—that had been staring at my lips—widened and flicked up to mine, a sliver of worry burning within. I knew exactly what thoughts crossed her mind; was it Kazan, the human painter she'd been falling for or the Mistwalker controlling him? I held her gaze, leaving her to wonder at her unspoken question. Over the next three weeks, before the rise of the next Mist, I would be planting more and more such hints until she could no longer deny the truth she instinctively knew but deliberately hid from.

"Come," I said, leading her towards the working area. "I can't wait to start painting you."

The slight trembling of her hand revealed the extent of her nerves and excitement, both of which echoed mine. I'd already set up the props for our first scene. Her gaze lingered on the three cameras set on tripods aimed at the dark-red Roman bed with beige, intricately patterned legs and cushions of matching color, golden tassels at each corner. It had no backrest but slightly recurved on one end. Before it stood a small stepping stool with the same beige cushion on top, which could also serve as a low bench. Off to the side, next to a black and white folding screen, I'd laid out on a table four different diaphanous, negligee and thong sets; black, blue, white, and red.

"I would like you to try each of these on, and then we'll pose you and take some pictures to choose the best outfit and angle."

She nodded, but I didn't miss her apprehensive look towards the cameras. I didn't sense any mistrust from her towards me, but her worry totally made sense. In this digital day and age, one never knew where pictures—especially suggestive or compromising ones—could end up, even more so when taken by strangers or someone you barely knew.

"How I normally work with my other models is that I choose one to three shots from a given angle which I print in a large format then delete all the pictures. The rare pictures I preserve are always with the consent of the model," I explained, eager to reassure her. "If you're not comfortable with the pictures, I can simply sketch instead. I want you to be…"

Jade placed two fingers on my lips to silence me.

"It's okay. I'm a little paranoid about having my picture taken in skimpy outfits, but I do trust you. Plus, you've been around long enough without any scandals from your previous models, who were far hotter than me. So…" she said with a shrug.

"In my eyes, no one is hotter than you, my Jade."

A lovely shade of pink rose on her cheeks. I didn't think

she'd been fishing for a compliment, but I loved watching her blush.

"I forgot to show you the bathroom or offer you something to drink," I said, feeling sheepish. "Have you even had breakfast?"

"Don't worry," she said with an indulgent smile. "I'm well fed. However, a sip of water and a pit stop would be welcome before we get started."

"Right away, Milady," I said with a flourishing curtsey.

I showed her the bathroom located at the back of the living-room, between the two bedrooms. Leaving her to it, I went to the kitchen to get us some water.

Jade came out a few moments later, having taken a minute to fix her hair. Little did she know I intended to mess it up very soon.

"You can change behind the screen," I said, pointing at it with my index finger. "On the other side, the panels are all mirrors. There's a bench behind it as well to put your clothes on, but I can bring a clothes rack if you prefer."

"No, no, that's fine," she said, her nerves coming back with a vengeance.

She walked hastily towards the table and grabbed the black set before disappearing behind the folding screen. I couldn't tell if the need to hide or the fear of losing her nerve had prompted Jade into moving so quickly.

While my mate changed, I fetched a sketchbook and a pencil, then a tall stool to sit on while drawing. My heart all but stopped beating when she stepped out from behind the screen. The sheer, black lace over her round, perky breasts left little to the imagina-tion, yet hid enough to make you want to tear it off. The diaphanous dress barely veiled her delicious hourglass figure, or the slim triangle of the black thong. The lacy hem of the negligee caressed her thighs with each hesitant step, the open slit in the middle giving little winks of bare skin.

I swallowed hard and forced myself to snap out of my lustful daze.

"You are perfect," I said, my voice gravelly with desire.

"Where do you want me?" Jade asked, tucking a strand of her lustrous red hair behind her ear in a self-conscious gesture.

In my bed, writhing beneath me, and screaming my name.

"Here, let me show you," I said, squelching my rabid hunger and the deviant thoughts racing through my mind.

Placing my hand on the small of her back, I gently nudged her towards the Roman bed. I held her hand while she stepped up on the small bench to climb onto the bed, giving me a most wonderful view of her rear. From behind, the string thong gave the impression she had no underwear. She sat down, facing me, eyes wide, her pulse racing in her neck.

"Lie down, love," I said, helping her get her legs up as she complied.

She scooted up a little so that her head rested more comfortably on the raised end of the narrow bed. I made her turn slightly on her side so her body partially faced towards me.

"Place your right arm over your head and let your left arm rest lazily over your stomach."

Jade obeyed, letting me adjust the pose. My hand trailed down the length of her shapely legs before I made her part them, bending them a bit at the knee. I smiled, staring at her bare feet, the nail polish on her toes almost perfectly matching the dark red of the bed. Parting the skirt of her negligee, I let one pane dangle over the edge of the bed and the other fall behind her back, exposing the luminescent skin of her flat belly, and her adorable navel. With the back of my hand, I caressed the bare flesh of her stomach, which quivered beneath my touch. Jade's breath caught in her throat as I lowered the string of her thong to the side of her hip. I took a step back to admire her pose, then approached again to make some adjustments. The final touch consisted of splaying her hair out over the headrest, artistically allowing some of it to cascade down the bed or over her shoulder and onto her chest.

I locked eyes with her as my hand carefully slipped under the shoulder string, sliding it down to bare her left breast enough to show a nipple. Her stunning green eyes darkened, and her pupils dilated as my hand covered her breast. I fondled it gently before thumbing its little bud until it hardened. Lifting my hand, I repressed a smile at her disappointed look and arranged her hair around her nipple, making it stand out further.

Leaning over Jade, a hand on each side of her head, I brushed my lips against hers. "Don't move," I said before kissing her again, deeply.

My cock throbbed with desire, and I fisted the cushion, savoring her for a few seconds longer before breaking the kiss.

"Think naughty thoughts," I said against her lips, then kissed her again. "Focus on your wildest fantasy, your kinkiest wet dream. I want to see the face of a woman consumed with passion. By the time I start sketching, I want you soaking wet. Don't be self-conscious. Moan if you need to but show me your fire."

I kissed her one last time then straightened up to admire my woman's beauty. As I turned to leave, she whispered my name.

"Kazan... Who is he? Who is my demon?" Jade asked, her voice sultry with arousal.

I hesitated for a second. Forcing a neutral expression on my face, I said, "I believe you already know, Jade. I believe you're already thinking about him, and the decadent things you love him doing to you."

A troubled expression crossed her beautiful features while a slight blush spread over her face and chest. I wondered how long before she acknowledged her growing suspicions.

"Let him have his way with you," I whispered before bending down and nipping her exposed nipple, hard enough to draw a hiss of pleasure-pain from her.

I straightened up, turned around, and walked out of the cameras' frames without giving her a chance to respond. Using the remote linked with all three cameras on the tripods, I took a few shots, then approached her with a fourth handheld camera to take a few top down shots and a few more at odd angles. Grabbing my sketchbook, I settled on the stool and burned through a dozen pages of sketches, stopping occasionally to modify her pose, allow Jade to change her outfit, take more pictures, and sketch some more.

Jade did moan a few times, the heady scent of her arousal making me dizzy at times. Had I been in my ethereal form, it would have driven me insane. Thankfully, the human vessel's stunted sense of smell only perceived a fraction of it, dimming its potency and, therefore, its power over me.

Time flew by. A little over three hours had lapsed since we started. Jade had not complained but in the last hour, she'd increasingly broadcast feelings of sleepiness and hunger. I called a lunch break, which she greatly appreciated. I had offered her breaks previously which she had declined, not wanting to ruin the pose.

"Let's order in," I proposed while helping her off the bed. The image of a platter of dumplings, which flashed through my mind, came from her. "What do you want to eat?" I asked. "There's a very nice Chinese place nearby that delivers. They could be here in less than twenty minutes."

Jade beamed at me. "I was just thinking about some dumplings!"

"Great minds think alike," I said, not feeling deceitful in the least. It was my duty to please my woman by whatever means necessary. "Come," I said, wrapping my arm around her shoulders. "Let's go check out the menu."

She instinctively wrapped her arm around my waist but somewhat resisted when I led her towards the door to the kitchen.

"Shouldn't I change first?" she asked, looking down at her barely veiled body.

"I'd rather you didn't. The view is far too lovely," I said, shamelessly. "Don't worry, the delivery guy won't see you."

She huffed and shook her head at me, disbelieving. "That's not really fair. Where's my eye candy?"

I burst out laughing, not having expected that comeback.

"Fair enough," I said, releasing her shoulders. Grabbing the hem of my white shirt, I lifted it up and over my head before balling it in my fist. Chest and feet bare, my charcoal cargo shorts constituted my only remaining garment. "Better?" I asked.

Jade's jaw dropped, and she stared at me, wide-eyed. Her gaze roamed over my muscular chest, lingering on my eight-pack. She licked her lips nervously then nodded her head.

"Yes," she said with a thin voice.

"Good! Now, let's get you fed," I said, tucking her under my arm again.

We padded into the kitchen, and I retrieved the menu from one of the drawers before handing it over to her. I pulled out one of the cushioned wooden chairs from around the table and gestured for her to take a seat.

"Pick what you want, and we'll order enough for two. I'm fine with anything so follow your heart's desires. I'll be right back with the cameras."

"Okay," she said before flipping through the menu, her hunger steadily growing.

By the time I returned, she already had an impressive list chosen. A quick call later, our food was ordered. After laying down the four cameras on the coffee table in the living room, I lured Jade to the couch and sat her on my lap. She gave a token protest before settling on me. The urge to drag her to my bedroom came back with a fury, but I reined it in.

"Grab one of the cameras, love," I said while turning on the giant screen.

When she handed it over to me, I projected the images onto my Smart TV via the Wi-Fi connection before passing it back to her to scroll through the photos I'd taken. Arms wrapped around her midsection, I nuzzled her nape and absentmindedly caressed her stomach with my thumbs through the parted panes of her negligee.

Too soon for me, but at long last for her, the delivery man arrived. I laid down the food on the coffee table and fetched us plates. Jade dove in, moaning in delight as she sampled bits of the various dishes.

I envied her enthusiasm.

While my human vessel required sustenance, I struggled with mortal food. In the Mist Plane, I'd always enjoyed any food Jade had wanted, but here, things were different. The human taste buds left no room to imagination or the slightest wiggle room. You either liked it or hated it.

My woman had a sweet tooth.

All the things she loved contained excessive sugar. That Sangria last night contained at least two pounds of sugar, the ribs twice as much, and ditto with the chicken wings. The butter on the popcorn, ugh… Might as well have chugged down a bottle of oil. And this Chinese food… On top of the oiliness of all the deep-fried foods, they also happened to be soaking in overly sweet sauces of some kind. The dumplings—without the far too salty soy sauce—the beef and broccoli with steamed rice, and the sautéed vegetables saved me.

At least, art-wise, we were on the same page.

While I didn't allow her to look at my sketches, far too revealing as to who her 'demon' was, we quickly agreed on three pictures as our favorites, discarding the others. By the time we returned to work, something had shifted between us. I doubted Jade realized it, but her subconscious was putting two and two together and making its peace with it.

Soon, my Jade. Soon.

CHAPTER 5
JADE

After the painful breakup with Patrick three years ago, if anyone had told me I'd get back on the dating scene by getting involved with the fabulous Kazan Dale—who also, likely, happened to be occasionally possessed by the Mistwalker who was obsessed with me—I would have had them committed. Over the past couple of weeks since our first meeting, my boyfriend had dropped a number of hints, some not so subtle, that implied he was aware of the Mistwalker's presence.

I didn't understand how my 'monster' could cross into our world without the Mist and suspected it required a lot of energy. That would explain why he only rarely manifested himself physically, except for that one undeniable time when he did so to defend us from the thugs on my first date with Kazan. But most incidents had only been the tingling sensation and occasionally the painful throb. Fortunately, I couldn't remember the latter occurring more than a couple of times. At first, I'd thought it to be a jealous fit from the Mistwalker to separate me from Kazan. But now, I believed he'd been leeching energy from me to keep himself anchored in our world.

Kazan had swept me off my feet. He was everything I'd ever

dreamt of. So perfect... Too perfect. You'd think someone had taken my list of the ideal man and checked every box while putting him together. And yet, something felt off. Obviously, having some otherworldly being taking control of him was messed up enough, but his acceptance of it disturbed me. Being too much of a coward, I hadn't confronted him about it yet, but we needed to address the elephant in the room.

Part of me hoped my paranoia had me seeing things that weren't there and another wanted it to be true. To my shame, the idea of having a monster as a life mate had me beyond excited. When Kazan had shown me his collection the first time, I'd been grateful for the chance to go to the bathroom before wearing the sexy outfit he'd prepared for me because I'd been soaking wet. Every single painting had reflected one of my deepest fantasies. Part of me wanted to be the beauty to Kazan's beast, but only if HE was the beast. I didn't want a third-party entity to take possession of his body and snuff out Kazan, not only because I was falling hard and fast for him, but also because no human being deserved such a fate.

The phone rang, startling me from my somber thoughts. Picking it up from the patio table, I rose to my feet and went back inside as I answered. Laura had poked her friends with more questions from me, and I didn't want indiscreet ears to eavesdrop on that rather sensitive conversation.

"Hey Sis!" I said, heading for the living-room and letting myself drop into my lazy-boy.

"Hey Jade," Laura said with her usual bubbly enthusiasm. "How are you? And more importantly, how is drop-dead-sexy-and-mysterious doing?"

I laughed at her silliness. "Kazan is doing great. We're going shopping later today. He wants a few new clothes for himself and a lot more babydolls, garter belts and other sexy outfits for me."

I didn't mention chains, collars and shackles for one specific scene.

"More?!" she exclaimed, disbelieving. "Didn't he already get you a full wardrobe of them?"

My face heated. "Yeah, but they kind of went through a bit of a rough time. He had to tear them up so that I looked like I'd been attacked by something wild."

"Man, I can't wait to see those paintings," Laura said in awe.

"That makes two of us. He won't let me see anything until it's the right time," I said, pouting.

"Artists, you're all the same," she said mockingly. "Serves you right to get a taste of your own medicine."

I harrumphed in annoyance. It's true that I didn't like showing people my work in progress, but I'd been getting better. No choice in my line of work. Despite being the Lead Artist on my game, if the Creative Director or Art Director demanded to see what I'd been working on, they wouldn't tolerate me displaying any kind of diva reluctance.

"So? Give me the goods," she said in a conspiratorial tone. "Is he as beastly as his paintings?"

I gasped and rolled my eyes at Laura's typical inappropriate prying. Granted, she had zero problem volunteering far too many details about the sexual prowess of whichever jock she was currently involved with, but I'd never been the type to kiss and tell. That didn't stop her from trying.

"First off, it's none of your business, and second, there's nothing to tell," I said in a clipped tone.

"Nothing to tell? As in your selfish ass won't share or you guys still haven't done it?"

My hesitation while trying to give a noncommittal answer gave me away.

"Oh my God, you still haven't!" she exclaimed. "What the hell? Why?"

"We've only been dating two weeks!" I said defensively.

"Two weeks is more than enough time, not to mention you've spent the majority of that time sprawled mostly naked in lascivious poses with him happily groping you and copping a feel left, right, and *center*," she countered in her trademark 'don't give me that BS' tone. "What's the problem? Do I need to prescribe him some blue pills?"

I snorted at that ridiculous question. Kazan and I had been doing some seriously heavy petting over the past two weeks. More than once during our painting sessions, his cock had strained so much against his pants, I'd half expected the zipper to tear open. The way he looked at me like a starving man, I didn't quite understand why he hadn't ravaged me like he clearly wanted to.

"First off, you can't write prescriptions yet. And second, believe me, that man doesn't need any kind of help in that department. His equipment has no problem whatsoever to stand at the ready," I said, unable to resist defending my man's virility.

"So, what's the hang up? You're overdue to dust the cobwebs you've got down there. How long has it been? Three years?"

I shook my head at the phone, speechless. "Jees, Laura. Can you be any more crude? This isn't about scratching some itch. I really like this guy, I mean REALLY like him, and the Mist-walker business is ruining it for me." Sudden tears pricked my eyes as I got choked up on the last words. "I don't want him to hurt Kazan, and I need to know which of the two will be lying in bed with me. Whenever Kazan and I get close, the Mistwalker lurks nearby. And sometimes I can even feel him touching me, not physically, but on a psychic level, if that makes any sense. And it shames me because I actually like it. But that's cheating, isn't it? I can't make him go away. Each passing day, his pres-ence feels stronger. I fear he's taking over Kazan."

"I'm sorry," Laura said, finally understanding the depth of my distress. "I didn't realize it had gotten this complicated. I asked Richard about the whole possession thing, and he said all his research and people he talked to came to the same conclusion that there's no such thing."

"But I saw him all wrapped around Kazan, lending him his strength during that fight," I argued. "Sometimes, I could swear I'm seeing the Mistwalker almost like an aura around him."

"You said it yourself, sweetie, he was *wrapped around* him, and *lending* him his strength. He wasn't him. Maybe he's just shadowing him, like an aura. Honestly, the only way to solve this is to ask him directly. You've always been the one telling me to just take the bull by the horns."

Kicking my slippers off, I raised my feet, hugging my knees to my chest.

"If I'm wrong, he'll think I'm crazy," I said in a small voice. "Hey Kazan, are you possessed by the Mistwalker who's stalking me and has been giving me crazy wet dreams?" I snorted again. "He'll kick me out of his place, lock the doors, and get a restraining order on my ass."

Laura chuckled. "There's direct and then there's direct, silly goose. You want to ease him into it. Come in through the backdoor. Find some analogy and get him to express his views on it. You're the nerd. Surely there's some sci-fi or paranormal movie where you have some human possessed by another creature or sharing his consciousness with some parasitic being. Ask him how he'd feel in that human's shoes. If he's 'possessed' by the Mistwalker, he'll know exactly where you're coming from. If he's not, you save face by simply having a theoretical conversation."

I remained speechless for a moment, blown away by the simplicity of the solution. This was not only perfect, I even knew which TV show and character to reference.

"When did you grow this wise?" I asked, pleasantly surprised and particularly grateful.

"My big sister's endless speeches on getting my shit together are finally sinking in," she said in a teasing, but affectionate, tone.

"I love you, you little brat."

"I love you, too, old hag."

~

K azan showed up at my house five minutes early. I'd
spent too much time talking with Laura as she updated
me on the wild parties on campus, while reassuring me her
studies still came first. Then I'd spent another ridiculous amount
of time fixing both my toenails and fingernails. As a result, I
was still scrambling to finish getting ready. Thankfully, Kazan
had elected to lease a rental car for the month to see if it proved
more convenient than a cab for our numerous activities. It also
made better financial sense, which made me feel all the more
guilty that he did all the spending whenever we went out.
Although I didn't live paycheck to paycheck, my tight budget
only allowed me a handful of outings each month. According to
Kazan, it was no burden for him, but I didn't want him thinking
me a gold-digger or social climber. I wanted a boyfriend, not a
sugar daddy.

As per usual, he stood outside by the car waiting for me. I
waved him in, my hair still not fully done. He hopped back into
the car—a sleek, burnished silver Jaguar—to turn off the engine
then sauntered up to the porch. Kazan stopped outside the door,
giving me an intense stare as if needing me to confirm I truly
wanted him to enter.

"Come in, babe," I said, waving him in again. "I'm sorry for
being late. Give me two minutes to finish drying my hair and put
some shoes on."

He stepped inside, pulled me into his embrace, and gave me
a searing kiss that made me reconsider our plans to go shopping
after all. Releasing me, his gaze roamed over the décor. It made
me feel self-conscious. Despite the subdued colors of the off-
white walls, with darker brown furniture, and some red and blue
accents on the pillows and wall paintings—some of them my

own—my house felt warm and welcoming, not cheap but nowhere near fancy.

"Please make yourself at home," I said tucking a wet strand of hair behind my ear. "Feel free to look around. The kitchen is right there if you want something to drink. My office studio is in the back. I won't be long."

He nodded with a smile, and I raced up the stairs to the bathroom where I made quick work of drying my hair, letting it cascade over my white crop top. I applied some nude lip gloss, and stuffed my feet into comfortable, white sneakers. I usually wore medium heels with the black leggings I had on, but it wasn't a good idea for pounding the pavement while shopping.

I came downstairs and found Kazan walking slowly into my office. He examined every single nook and cranny of the house as if trying to memorize every inch of it or seeking the answer to a lifelong mystery. There was something solemn in the way in which he gazed upon everything.

It's like he's just entered a sacred shrine.

Which made absolutely no sense. Many things about Kazan didn't quite make sense, but I considered them endearing little quirks. I observed him quietly while he completed his tour. Beneath his veneer of class and elegance, everything about him screamed virility, strength, and even a slight sense of danger. Yet, he projected such a powerful aura of innocence. Even now, as he turned to face me, his eyes shone with the wonder of a child presented with the best toy he had ever dreamed of. My chest tightened with an emotion I couldn't put into words.

"Your house is the perfect reflection of you. Complex in its simplicity, beautiful, warm, inviting with a treasure trove of exciting stories to tell. I love it."

"I'm glad you do," I said, deeply moved. "I have a feeling you'll be spending a lot of time here in the future. You're welcome anytime."

Drawing me once more into his embrace, he kissed me, this

time with none of the lustful passion from when he first arrived. It was tender, loving, and almost reverent. It brought tears to my eyes. After he broke the kiss, he held me tight. I buried my face in his neck, enjoying the closeness and intimacy of the moment. Something settled in my chest, even as the tingle of the Mist-walker timidly manifested itself at the back of my nape.

Kazan released me only to take my hand and lead me out of the house. Always the gentleman, he held the door for me while I got into the Jag and closed it for me before going around to the driver's seat. He buckled his seatbelt, started the car, checked his blind spot, then took off. I bit back a smile. As much as his art pushed the boundaries of monster erotica, he handled everything else in his life by the book.

He let go of the steering wheel with one hand to grab mine and put it on his lap. I loved it when he placed his hand on my own thigh. Something about the possessiveness of the gesture, this reassertion of his claim did wondrous things to me. But I loved even more that he'd placed my hand on his thigh, which translated to me as a reminder that he had freely given himself to me; he was mine.

Kazan didn't turn on the radio. I couldn't recall ever hearing him play any music. It didn't actually bother me, but it added yet another layer of mystery to my man. Although we did exchange snippets of conversation, we mostly remained in an amicable silence, each of us lost in thought. The ride almost felt too short as we pulled up to the shopping mall. As expected on an early Friday evening, the place was packed. Ever the gentleman, Kazan dropped me in front of the door while he went on the hunt for a parking spot. He'd catch up with me in the lingerie store.

As his car turned into one of the parking rows, I noticed a suspiciously familiar black car following in his wake. It sounded paranoid, but I could swear I'd been seeing that same car quite often lately while on my way to or from work, while doing the grocery shopping or even lurking around in my neighborhood. It didn't make any sense though. Who could possibly want to stalk me and for what purpose?

Dismissing the somber thoughts, I entered the mall and made a beeline for Victoria's Secret. Laura had been right about her cobweb comment. I hadn't refreshed my sexy outfit collection in over three years. Things would—hopefully—soon move on to the next stage with Kazan. I didn't want to be caught in granny panties when we finally got around to bumping uglies.

As I browsed through the naughtily divine pieces, the nagging feeling of being observed returned in earnest. Lifting my head, I looked around but didn't find anyone staring. Yet, even as I shrugged it off, the sensation didn't fade. The third time I gazed up, I spotted a familiar-looking man turning away. I couldn't swear he was the same person, but I'd been noticing someone eerily similar in random crowds around me as I went about my business these last couple of weeks. He was always clad in dark clothes, usually wearing some kind of a hat from baseball cap to beanie, often with sunglasses. This man wore a flat cap and regular glasses.

Good God! I'm totally losing it.

In his late twenties, early thirties, a bit of a hipster style, he was probably hunting some gift for his wife or girlfriend. Dismissing him from my thoughts, I forced myself to ignore my unease and grabbed a few pieces before hurrying to the cash register. I didn't want Kazan to see them until I modeled them for him. Having already bought from the same lines previously, I didn't doubt they would fit.

The cashier did quick work of wrapping up the thongs, including a very naughty maid set. The bra had zero fabric over the breasts, only lacy frills circling them, with a white lace choker and a barely there, black and white, transparent mini skirt. I had considered buying a similar set, S&M themed, in the last days of my relationship with Patrick in an ultimate, desperate effort to rekindle the flame between us, but I'd thought better of it. You couldn't keep a man with sex alone, even less so if his heart already belonged to another.

Kazan walked up to me and slipped his arm around my waist, his thumb caressing the exposed skin below my crop top.

"What did you get?" he asked, trying to peer into the bag after the cashier handed it over to me.

I hid it behind my back, giving him a falsely stern look. "All in due time... Assuming I even let you see them."

"What?" he exclaimed, looking at me like I'd just stolen his favorite toy.

"If you're a good boy, I might consider it."

"I'm always good," he mumbled, leading me out of the shop.

We headed to the basement of the mall, which gave access to a tiny parking lot where only two shops operated: the shoe repair store and on the opposite side, mostly hidden by the escalator, the erotic boutique Dungeon Mistress. Before meeting Kazan, I'd never set foot inside that place, being far too shy and self-conscious. But now, I sauntered right in without any shame. Having Kazan by my side made me bolder and more confident. I couldn't explain why, but I loved it.

It was my third trip here and my eyes still popped at all the kinky paraphernalia, from dominatrix leather outfits to edible underwear, floggers to whips, canes to paddles, ropes and chains. The owner dedicated a full wall to shackles and bonding devices, another with the craziest collection of dildos and vibrators, and numerous shelves and displays near the cashier offered every-thing else including massaging oils, lubricants, batteries, and erotic literature and movies. A back room contained larger appa-ratus and bondage furniture like a Saint Andrew's Cross, bondage benches, spanking horses, and even a gynecological chair.

Kazan informed me that the owner, a plump older lady who looked like anyone's eccentric aunt, had told him he could come in any time with a model to take pictures or sketch using the erotic furniture. The look in his eyes when he said it hinted he had such plans for me in the not too distant future. That got me instantly hot and bothered.

Without hesitation, Kazan made a beeline for the chains, choosing a dark-grey one with thick chain links. He looked at different metal collars, clasping them around my neck to find the perfect one, then did the same with wrist and ankle shackles. To my surprise, I found myself putting on a show for the other patrons whenever I caught them spying on us, quite a few of them with undisguised interest in Kazan.

He's all mine, bitches. Keep drooling.

He selected one smaller chain then a few leather bustiers and thongs, and a couple sets of erotic lingerie that qualified more as strings than clothing. The owner, Lorna, oohed and aahed at the items Kazan laid out on the counter. She gave him a very sugges-tive once over, not hiding her appreciation in the least. Instead of offending me, it made me laugh. Lorna winked at me before scanning our items. As she placed the last one in the bag, she reached for a colorful little box next to the cash register.

"Want some cherry flavored condoms?" she asked, waving the box before us. "They're on sale."

I gaped at her before casting a sideways glance at Kazan. He once again had that blank look he often got when asked ques-tions he had no clear answers for. It troubled me. Sometimes, I wondered if he suffered from some mild form of autism or if something else was the cause.

Looking back at the box, I hesitated. We hadn't had sex yet, but I firmly believed that would be rectified within the next couple of days. My contraceptive implant had another six months or so left on it, but I'd been considering replacing it early to avoid any surprises. I was clean and felt certain that Kazan was as well. But being extra cautious couldn't hurt.

"They're magnum," Lorna added, wiggling her brows at Kazan.

I snorted, grabbed the box from her hand, and tossed it into our bag. She chuckled, grabbed a second box, scanned it then tossed it in the bag as well.

"It's two for the price of one with total purchases of over fifty dollars," she said with a grin. "The edible underwear will be on sale next week. You can grab some when you come back to restock on the condoms."

I burst out laughing and grabbed the bag she was extending towards us.

"Thanks, Lorna," I said, dragging Kazan after me.

Two packs of twelve… Twenty-four condoms in one week… As if…

And yet, that'd be three times a day for eight days. The first time we'd have sex, I expected to go through at least five rounds with him.

Maybe we will need them after all!

I chuckled inwardly at my naughty thoughts as we stepped onto the escalator. Turning to face him, the intensity of his stare threw me. His stormy eyes had darkened, and his expression reminded me of that of a predator… a hungry predator.

"They were on sale," I said with a playful shrug to ease the tension.

Kazan didn't respond. Instead, he slipped his hand behind my nape and drew my face to his before kissing me with a possessiveness and passion that left me weak in the knees.

Oh yeah, we'd be using these soon.

He seemed as frustrated as I felt that we still had his shopping to do, both of our minds having taken a deep dive into the gutter. With his usual chivalrous ways, Kazan carried all of our bags as we strolled around the mall on our way to Shay & Vincent, a posh men's wear boutique with extremely varied merchandise. Once again, Kazan headed straight to a specific section of the store which contained the fancy version of biker wear, yet I didn't miss how his eyes lingered on completely different sections of the store containing the same kind of clothes that had seemed to draw his attention from other shops on our way here.

Kazan browsed through the clothes with an indifference that baffled me. Whatever I said looked nice, he would immediately look for one in his size even though he, personally, didn't seem particularly taken with that piece or any other for that matter. To my dismay, I realized that my man's godly body proved quite the nightmare when it came to buying off the rack. His broad shoulders and muscular arms made it nearly impossible to find anything that wouldn't look on the verge of bursting on him. Sure, it made him look ridiculously sexy the way the clothes molded his sculpted body, but it had to be uncomfortable.

When I dragged him over to the boho, retro punk section, his face lit up. He tried to hide his sudden enthusiasm but failed miserably. It proved a painstaking process nonetheless, finding a few pieces that fit him properly and looked sexy on him. The hardest part was not to burst out laughing when some shirts, too short at the hem or in the sleeves made him resemble a dressed gorilla. He started making a game of it, deliberately grabbing things that would make himself look ridiculous and acting falsely outraged when I failed to hide my hilarity. He actually had me roaring with laughter and begging for mercy before he stopped being a goober. I walked out of the shop with a newfound respect for the plight of muscular men, right up there with big breasted women who couldn't wear a single blouse without the buttons all but popping open.

While I liked the biker, bad boy style Kazan usually wore, I had to admit the bohemian style fit him beautifully. The low necks or open shirts and leather necklaces with the pendant resting on his muscular chest was beyond sexy. But above all, it made him feel good.

On our way back to the car, the sense of being watched hit me with renewed vigor. Stopping dead in my tracks, I turned around abruptly to look behind us. Kazan, both hands burdened with our purchases, stopped as well and looked at me questioningly before following my gaze. The same man with the flat cap was hastily walking away. I knew he'd been staring at us.

"Who is he?" Kazan asked, a sliver of tension in his voice.

"I don't know," I said, honestly. "But I think he's been following me. He was looking at me in the lingerie shop, and when you went off to park the car, I saw a black car following you that resembles one I've been seeing pretty often lately. I guess the driver dropped him off so he could spy on me while he looked for a parking spot, too." Kazan's expression hardened with each of my words. "Do you know who he is?"

"I don't know them," he said after a beat. "The next time you see them following you, I want you to go to the most public place in the vicinity and call me immediately."

I nodded, suddenly feeling frazzled. Shifting all the bags to one hand—which had to be painful seeing how much they weighed—Kazan wrapped his freed arm around me, tucking me against him.

"Do not be afraid, my Jade. No one will hurt you."

I shuddered at the eerie similitude of his words to those of the Mistwalker. Yet, I didn't sense the presence of the ethereal being or feel the tingling usually associated with him. Kazan tightened his embrace and hurried us to the car.

Although he tried to lighten the mood with casual conversation on the way back to my house, I didn't miss the careful and frequent way he glanced at the rearview and side mirrors as he drove, no doubt on the lookout for any pursuers. I did my fair share of checking the passenger side mirror for any signs of the black car, in vain. By the time we rolled up to my house, we were both a lot more relaxed.

Mr. and Mrs. Palmer, once more hanging out on their front porch, eyed my companion with blatant curiosity. Mrs. Palmer's gaze lingered on the bags in Kazan's hands. Despite the bright street lights, night had already fallen, making it harder for the nosy woman to get a good view of the labels. Thankfully, the Dungeon Mistress bag was mostly hidden by the Victoria's Secret one. I wished he had brought out his Shay & Vincent bags instead, but I could deal with being outed for wearing sexy lingerie rather than for kinky equipment.

We nodded at them on our way to my house. Her barely repressed smile told me she'd not only give me the third degree the next time we spoke, but that she'd also be talking her poor husband's ears off with wild speculations.

I closed the door behind us, and Kazan deposited the bags on the dining table, looking amused.

"Have I ruined your reputation?" he asked, mockingly.

"I believe so. You'd better prepare to battle to restore my honor, oh valiant warrior," I said wrapping my arms around his neck.

"I'll fight the Gods and the Titans themselves to defend your honor, my beloved," he said against my lips before kissing me.

I melted against him, but he put an end to it, all too soon.

"Are you hungry?" I asked as he pulled away from me. "I've got some steaks in the fridge. I could make a salad or rice with steamed veggies if you'd like? Or we could order in."

Kazan hesitated. He had started nodding, going along with one of my requests as usual, but held back. That pleasantly surprised me.

"Actually, I'm not hungry but I'll be glad to steal a couple of bites from your plate."

I smiled. "In truth, I'm actually not hungry either since I ate before you picked me up."

"We're all good then," he said, smiling as well.

"All right. Let me go put this upstairs, and you can take the shots you wanted in the panic room's staircase," I said, getting excited at the thought of posing for him again.

I grabbed the Victoria's Secret bag and quickly rummaged in the Dungeon Mistress bag to remove one of the condom boxes.

"Where are you taking that?" Kazan asked before I could discreetly slip it into the lingerie bag.

My face heated, and I licked my lips nervously. "Taking one upstairs?"

"Why?" he asked, his stare intense.

"So that we have one here and the other at your place for... you know... when we need it."

Kazan took a few steps towards me, closing the distance between us. My breath caught in my throat as his eyes darkened.

"When will we need it?" he whispered.

I swallowed hard, my gaze dropping to his sensuous lips. "Technically, we don't need them since I have a contraceptive implant," I said, absentmindedly touching the skin of my arm which covered it. "I'm clean, and I'm assuming you are, too?"

"I am."

"But they're cherry flavored, so... I guess that counts for something?"

God, I felt so clumsy and juvenile. You'd think I was eighteen, not twenty-eight.

"Would you let me make love to you, Jade?"

My heart skipped a beat, and I couldn't seem to draw in enough oxygen. Voicelessly, I nodded my assent.

"Right here? Right now?" he persisted, moving even closer to me.

I nodded again, unable to speak, hypnotized by his stormy eyes.

"Do you want me as much as I want you, Jade?"

"Yes, Kazan. I do."

He drew me to him. Clasping my hands behind his neck—the box making it somewhat awkward—I purred as his palms ran down my back before settling on my butt, and then lifting me up.

I instinctively wrapped my legs around him. His gaze locked with mine, he headed for the stairs up to my bedroom.

My pulse raced as he carefully laid me down on the bed. Staring me straight in the eyes, he slowly stripped out of his clothes. I blindly placed the box of condoms on the nightstand, almost dropping it to the floor as I feasted my eyes on my man's breathtaking perfection. At 6'7, with the muscle mass of a character straight out of an epic, demi-god warrior novel, a dreamy face, and mesmerizing eyes, Kazan embodied every fantasy I had ever held of the ideal man. My gaze never strayed from him as I kicked off my shoes and wiggled out of my leggings. Halfway through yanking off my socks, I watched him lower his pants, exposing his erect shaft. My jaw dropped, and my mind went numb. Long, thick, with ropy veins along its length, it qualified more as a club than a cock.

I gulped with a mixture of fear and excitement, my undies instantly drenched with my arousal. As he stepped out of his pants, I tossed my socks aside and reached for the hem of my crop top. Lifting it over my head, I squealed in surprise when Kazan's hands clasped around my ankles, dragging my bum to the edge of bed. Battling my way out of the crop top still covering my face, I yanked it off only to have it tangle in my hair.

My groan of frustration turned into a startled gasp as Kazan brushed his lips against the length of my inner thigh while kneeling before me, and then buried his face between my legs. A burning flame exploded in the pit of my stomach. He nuzzled me over the tiny triangle of my midnight blue thong, his hands roaming up and down my thighs, over my stomach, then back down my legs.

Breath laboring with anticipation and excitement, I absent-mindedly rid myself of the pesky top. Lifting my head, I looked at Kazan, his gorgeous face mostly concealed by his lustrous, wavy, black hair. My breath caught in my throat when he grabbed the side of my thong with his teeth and pulled it aside to expose me to him. Lifting my legs over his shoulders, he covered my mound with soft kisses before teasing the seam with his hot, wet tongue. I whispered his name as a bolt of pleasure zipped through me. With slow, deliberate movements, Kazan explored me with his mouth, tasting, teasing, and sucking. I writhed beneath his sensual ministrations, my hips gyrating with a will of their own.

My back arched off the bed when he slipped two fingers inside me, and his lips latched onto my clit. Fisting his silky hair with one hand, I slipped the other one under my bra, pinching my painfully hard nipple. Skin afire, I gave myself over to the raging inferno building inside me as Kazan accelerated the movement of his hand. As I neared the edge, the familiar tingle of the Mistwalker manifested itself, spreading all over my feverish body instead of focusing around my nape as per its usual.

A blinding light exploded before my eyes as I detonated. I screamed Kazan's name, my head rolling from side to side in the throes of passion. The tingling sensation intensified, heightening the sensitivity of my skin.

Through my haze, I heard the crinkling sound of a condom wrapper being ripped open. I cracked my eyes open to see Kazan standing before me in his glorious nakedness, a feral look on his face, the intensity in his dark eyes pinning me in place. He didn't break eye contact as he rolled on the condom, apparently oblivious of the ghostly, black tendrils hovering around him like shadowy flames.

The familiar fear, excitement, and guilt coursed through me. I crawled backwards, instinctively wanting to get away from my 'monster' and yet, also wanting to be captured.

"Kazan," I whispered, uncertain what I wanted to say but feeling I needed to warn him.

My words died in my throat as he grabbed my ankle again, stopping me from crawling away, and climbed on top of the bed.

"Stay still," he said, in a commanding voice that had me paralyzed. "You are mine, Jade."

Although I heard the words through my ears, I could have sworn that last sentence also resonated inside my head in the disembodied voice of the Mistwalker.

Kazan kneeled between my legs, his hungry gaze roaming over me with a possessiveness that left me breathless. His palms caressed a path up my thighs before grabbing the waist of my thong. In one powerful movement, he snapped the strings and ripped the underwear from me. I gasped, my pulse and breathing accelerating further.

"All mine," he growled before pressing his mouth to my core again and nipping my clit.

I emitted a strangled cry as another bolt of pleasure went off inside me. His hands and lips trailed a path up over my stomach to my chest. Pushing up my bra to free my breasts, he rubbed his face in the valley between them before kissing each one in turn. My hands clutched the comforter as his hands reached for my bra which met the same fate as my thong. I shuddered when his lips lingered over the Mistwalker's brand, his tongue slowly tracing the pattern with disturbing reverence. As his mouth continued to explore me, he licked my clavicle, kissed the curve of my shoulders, and nipped at the pulse in my neck.

"Touch me," he ordered.

I wanted to comply, but my eyes flicked to the dark aura of the Mistwalker around him.

"Look at me," Kazan said, in a stern voice that brooked no argument. My eyes immediately flicked back towards his. "All is well, my Jade. It's me, your Kazan. Stay with me. Focus on me." His knees spread my legs wider, and he pressed his rock-hard cock against my core. "Touch me, my Jade. I need your hands on me, my love."

Those last words broke through the haze of my fear. Despite the strong sense of the Mistwalker's presence, I drowned in the turbulent sky of Kazan's eyes. Letting go of the comforter, I placed my hands on his narrow waist, caressing a slow path along his sides, and up his strong, muscular back.

"Yes... Yes!" he hissed, his face tense with pleasure.

He leaned down and captured my lips as he pressed himself inside me. His massive cock slipped inside me inch by inch with slow thrusts while our hands explored and our mouths devoured.

"Tell me you're mine, Jade," Kazan whispered against my lips as he picked up the pace. "Tell me you belong to me."

Lost in a sea of pleasure, each stroke fanning another blaze spreading like wildfire within me, I could barely focus on anything other than the feel of his burning skin against mine, the powerful arms holding me, the fullness of his length spearing me, and his hot breath mingling with mine.

"I'm yours, Kazan," I slurred, between moans. "I'm all yours. Take all of me."

"My Jade..."

The words came out as a barely understandable growl as something seemed to snap inside him. Slipping both arms behind my knees, he spread me even wider and pounded into me. Nails digging into his back, I screamed his name as I climaxed for the second time. Before I could fully recover, he flipped us around and lowered me back onto his stiff cock. Too dazed to ride him, I pressed my palms to his chest for support, while he held me above him with both hands under my bum, and thrust up into me.

The shadowy flames of the Mistwalker aura around Kazan as he took me made the bed appear to be covered in a troubled, oily sea. But I ignored it, hypnotized by Kazan's face, contorted with pleasure. I gave myself over to my lover as another wave of ecstasy slowly built again within me.

"I'm going to come, Jade. I'm going to fucking come. Come with me, my love."

The urgency and commanding edge in his voice undid me. I threw my head back with a guttural cry as my orgasm swept me, my inner walls clamping down on him. Kazan slammed me down on his cock as he shouted his own release. His body shuddered as he rode the last waves of his climax, grinding his pelvis against mine.

I collapsed on top of him, destroyed. Kazan wrapped his arms around me in a bruising hold and pressed a passionate kiss on my forehead before placing my head in the crook of his neck.

"You own me, Jade. I am all yours, and I'm never letting you go."

My stomach flip-flopped at being thus claimed. I kissed his neck and held onto him tightly. The last man I had allowed myself to love, that I had devoted myself to, in the end had not wanted to be mine, let alone keep me.

Keep me, Kazan. And let me keep you.

CHAPTER 6

KAZAN

My Jade... She looked so peaceful in her sleep. I marveled at her beautiful, naked body draped in a curtain of red hair, splayed on the bed. How I ached to wake her up and ravish her again, but she needed rest. I barely repressed a snort thinking that we'd already used four condoms in a single night. Considering how thoroughly—and passionately—I'd worn her out, it came as no surprise that she'd sleep in. My woman wasn't an early bird to begin with. Good thing it was Saturday morning.

Grabbing my pants, I regretted not having brought in my Shay & Vincent's bag of new clothes. I hadn't planned on us having sex, let alone spending the night. I still couldn't believe the boldness with which Jade had just grabbed the condoms from Lorna. I'd have to thank the older lady the next time I visited Dungeon Mistress.

Slipping a couple of condoms into the pockets of the pants in my hand, I tried to ignore my stiffening cock at the thought of all the other ways I wanted to take my woman. I quietly went to the bathroom in the hallway and took a quick shower. Sensing that Jade would be waking soon, I went down to the kitchen and rummaged through the fridge to find the ingredients for pancakes. While flipping the first one, the shuffling sound of Jade's footsteps reached me. I smiled, my belly tightening with a pleasant feeling at the thought of seeing my woman again. Thrumming with impatience, I tried to silence the fear that she might decide it had been a mistake.

It would crush me.

While she showered, I cooked some ham and bacon, having found no sausages. I then proceeded to make a huge stack of pancakes and cut up some oranges. Jade's brisk steps came down the stairs and padded along the short hallway before she entered the kitchen. Barefoot, she wore only an oversized sports t-shirt which fell to mid-thigh, her lustrous hair still slightly damp.

"Hmmm, something smells good," she exclaimed, her eyes sparkling.

Relief flooded me as she sauntered towards me, wrapped her arms around my waist, and lifted her face expectantly. I gladly leaned forward and kissed her, holding her tightly against me.

"Good morning, sleepy head," I said, releasing her.

"Your fault," she said, without the slightest shame before slapping my butt. "I'm famished!" she said, peering at the food laid out on the table. "You, sir, are quite the keeper."

My chest warmed.

"Good," I said, pulling a chair for her. "I fully intend to be kept."

Her face melted with a tender expression that tugged at my heart. I wanted her to always look at me that way, and I'd do everything in my power to make sure she did.

I finished laying out the food and settled next to her as we dug in. I liked ham and bacon, although the latter could be a little too salty at times. The pancakes didn't faze me either way; they had an interesting texture. A dab of maple syrup on them actually tasted nice, but butter and drowned in syrup like my woman liked it made my stomach revolt. I watched her plop a huge square of butter on her pancakes and then look at my plate, ready to inflict the same treatment upon my stack. Normally, I would have allowed her to do so and pasted a grateful grin on my face, but as we would spend the rest of the day together, I didn't want to fight nausea while keeping my power in check.

Bracing for Jade's reaction, I gestured for her not to give me any, smiling gently to soften the rejection. To my surprise, and delight, it didn't upset her. In fact, she seemed both stunned and... pleased. My mate had taken to closely observing my reaction to every situation, which unnerved me. I'd assumed she was testing how compatible we were in our likes and dislikes. But now, I was starting to question that assumption.

We finished the meal with pleasant chatter, although I noticed Jade testing my tastes throughout the meal by offering me different combinations of things, from coffee with sugar and milk—when she knew I usually stuck to freshly pressed fruit juice or water, finding coffee too bitter—to whipped cream on my orange slices. She did make me cave in to a tiny amount of coffee in lots of hot milk, with a hint of sugar and cinnamon. Although a little strange to the taste, it was rather pleasant.

She called me a *Latte dude*. I could live with that.

With barely ten days left before the next Mist, we still had quite a bit of work to do to complete the collection, or rather, one final piece which she would model for me in the staircase of her panic room. But before we got to that, Jade insisted we watch one of her favorite old school TV shows. Spooning on her couch, we ended up watching two back-to-back episodes of Star Trek: Deep Space Nine. Although she tried to hide it, whenever the Lieutenant Commander Jadzia Dax would appear on screen, Jade would study my reaction to her. I had to repress a smile, guessing what thoughts crossed her mind and wondering how she would word her questions.

As the credits started rolling, Jade turned on her back to look at me, her dainty fingers tracing circles on my chest and around the areola of my nipple. Forcing myself to ignore how her touch resonated in my groin, I focused on her instead, bracing for the question I knew would come.

"I love Jadzia. She's beautiful and smart," Jade said, trying to sound casual. "But as much as I love Dax and the idea of a symbiont, I don't think I could do it."

"Do what?" I asked, playing dumb.

"Play host to another sentient being. Having them control part of my body and my thoughts. Knowing that I'd never be a single individual again. Wouldn't that bother you?"

"Depends," I answered truthfully, slightly unnerved by her intense stare. "I would object to being possessed by a demon or some kind of parasite, to be taken against my will. But in Jadzia's case, she not only chose to become a host, she studied and worked hard for years for that honor, and to be deemed worthy of Dax."

"But wouldn't you fear losing yourself, your identity, to that other being?" Jade persisted.

"Once again, it depends. In the case of Jadzia, while welcoming Dax did alter part of her personality, it didn't erase who she was. She always knew that would happen and embraced it. I can see the appeal of sharing the mind and experience of a being far older and wiser than me," I said, gently brushing her hair from her face then caressed her cheek with my thumb. "I wouldn't object to hosting a being who is fundamentally good and wise, who could make me a more enlightened version of myself, while still being me and able to pursue my own aspirations."

Jade looked troubled as she reflected on my words, then chewed her bottom lip, hesitating to ask her next question. I bit the insides of my cheeks to keep from smiling.

"What about relationships?" she asked, after a beat. "Wouldn't it bother you to have this other male entity inside you while you're being intimate with your woman?"

There it was, at last.

"As long as it was my body touching her, that I kept control of my thoughts, my emotions, and of my actions towards her, and that she knew without a doubt that it was me making love to her, then no, I wouldn't care." My hand caressing her cheek slipped down to her breast, pausing long enough for my thumb to flick her nipple, then trailing down to her stomach where it settled. "And if our roles were reversed, I'd feel the same way. As long as it was your hands on me and that you remained a conscious and willing participant to everything I did to you, without influence from that other being, I wouldn't care."

Jade's eyes flicked between mine, searching. I withstood her scrutiny without flinching.

"But if you were hosting such a being, and I was aware of it, wouldn't it be like I'm cheating?"

I chuckled and kissed her lips. "No, because we'd be one. He'd be an intrinsic part of me that I deliberately welcomed. You couldn't love him without loving me." My hand rose back to her breast which I kneaded slowly. "Me loving this perky breast of yours and giving it attention right now doesn't make me love your other breast any less, or any other parts of you."

It wasn't quite an appropriate comparison, but she got the gist, if only by the not so subtle way my gaze roamed over her.

She shivered, a different type of tension building inside of her. I loved how I could still easily read her emotions and, in this instant, her desires. Sliding my hand back down, I lifted the hem of her oversized shirt, going straight for gold. To my shock—and a pleasant one at that—Jade had gone commando, as I often did.

"Good girl," I whispered against her lips, as my fingers explored her folds, already getting wet for me.

Her lips parted with a sharp breath intake, her green eyes smoldering.

"I'm not giving you another excuse to tear my undies," she said, arching into me.

"Oh, my darling, I'm only just warming up," I said, grazing

84

her jawline with my teeth, my fingers dipping inside of her. "I'll buy you a trunk full of frilly undies just so that I can tear them right off of that scrumptious body of yours before I take you."

Jade shuddered again, her breathing accelerated as her hips moved in tandem with my tormenting hand.

"I need more," she moaned as I sucked on her earlobe. "I need you inside me. Take me, Kazan. Fuck me, hard."

Blood rushed to my groin and the primal need I always felt in her presence, but kept in check, came raging to the fore. Reluctantly pulling away from her, I grabbed a condom from my pocket and discarded my pants. She lay sprawled before me, legs spread, her oversized shirt bunched up above her breasts. The sight of her red, painted nails rubbing her clit, while her other hand reached for me to come to her, almost undid me.

I fumbled with the packet, fighting the urge to just throw myself on her and fuck her to oblivion.

"Kazan, now!" she pleaded. "It's okay. I've got an implant."

If you only knew how much I want to.

But it wasn't okay. Not unless she acknowledged my true nature and understood the consequences.

Focusing on the task at hand, I finally got the condom on. Leaning down, I slipped my arms under Jade's legs. Instead of lying on top of her, I lifted her up in my arms. She squealed in surprise and clasped her hands behind my neck to steady herself. Thanks to the ridiculously strong body she had bestowed upon me, and the otherworldly strength inherited from my ethereal form, Jade weighed nothing in my arms. Impaling her onto my stiff cock, I devoured her lips while pushing myself deeper and deeper into my woman.

Once fully sheathed, I rocked slowly back and forth, giving her a chance to adjust to my girth while reveling in the tight warmth of her squeezing me from all sides. For the woes and challenges this human vessel gave me, its sensitive response to intimate moments with my mate would never cease to enchant me.

I gradually increased the speed of my thrusts, spurred on by the encouragements of my woman, asking me to take her deeper, harder. Complying, I plowed into her with unbridled fury, the slapping sound of our flesh meeting and of her strangled cries playing as the sweetest music to my ears. Nine long years I'd ached to make her mine, to have her see me, want me, and touch me. I wanted to tear off that condom and fill her with both my mortal seed and ethereal essence, binding me to her in the Mortal Plane.

Her eyes widened as my ethereal aura expanded. What I wouldn't give to wrap her within it, to be all at once around and inside her. Jade's legs trembled, her eyes glazing over, and her nails digging into my shoulders as she rode the edge of her impending climax. Bending her backward, I pumped into her with a slight change to my angle until I pummeled her sweet spot with each stroke.

Jade unraveled, nearly toppling backwards. I pulled her back up against me, pressing her to my chest without slowing down my movements in and out of her. She felt so damn good. Liquid fire raged in my nether region and down my legs. The spasms of her inner walls clamping down on me in her throes of ecstasy demanded for me to come, but I wasn't ready yet. I still wanted her too much.

Putting her down on the couch, still buried balls deep inside her, I lifted one of her legs over my shoulder, not giving her time to fully come down from her high. I almost tore off her shirt, but with my own climax imminent, I slipped a hand between us and rubbed her clit as I thrust into her at a punishing pace.

"Again, my Jade," I said through gritted teeth. "Come for me again."

Jade's entire body shook as she slowly crested again. Then she threw her head back, her body seizing, her mouth open in a silent O. A lightning bolt struck at the base of my spine which felt like it might snap from the violence of my orgasm. I shredded my vocal chords screaming the name of my mate as my seed shot out into the condom.

Soon... Soon there would be no more barriers between us.

I continued to slowly pump in and out of my woman as our hearts and breaths settled. Covering her face with soft kisses, we held each other close, savoring the post-coital intimacy.

Lifting my head, I locked my gaze with hers. "I am yours, Jade. Don't you ever doubt that it's me, your Kazan, making love to you. Your body and all of your pleasure are mine. And soon, I hope, so will your heart be."

I hadn't expected to spend two nights at Jade's house, or for her to spend last night with me in my own flat. In spite of all our frolicking and spending quality time together, rediscovering one another, we'd still managed to make the sketches for the final piece, and I even got some painting done at the loft.

Things were falling into place much better than I had hoped. Although she'd convinced herself I was carrying some kind of mystical entity within me, Jade would come to terms with having a not-fully-human partner. In six more days, the Mist would rise, and then all would be clear. But I still needed to finish the collection. As much as I hated parting from Jade, her day job would give me the time I needed to get everything ready. I still needed to introduce her to Monica, my agent, who was hard at work setting up the exhibit and breathing down my neck, giving me hell for my usual secrecy.

The exhibit would take place exactly five days after the Mist. Monica would only see the actual pieces on Tuesday, three days prior to the event. In spite of her annoyance, she proved to be a good sport, performing marketing miracles with what little material I had consented to share with her. She naturally knew about Jade and was eager to meet her. I told her she would after the Mist. Monica didn't need me to go into further details to know I was hoping she'd help alleviate whatever lingering fears Jade might have about my nature.

Stopping at a red light while driving Jade to work, I turned my head to look at my mate and once more thanked whatever powers that had finally allowed me to beat the improbable odds of being with the woman I'd been created for.

As the light turned green and I resumed driving, something in my rearview mirror drew my attention. I couldn't quite figure out what had bothered me at first before a truck, turning at an intersection, revealed the black car that I had noticed a few times too many. Blinding rage surged within me, but I forced my expression to remain neutral so as not to alert Jade. Taking her hand, I lifted it to my lips and kissed her palm. She gave me a tender smile.

"Call me when you're ready for me to come pick you up," I said as we pulled into the parking lot of her studio. "I'll get you a key to my flat on my way home." Eyes wide, lips parted, Jade stared at me in shock. Leaning forward, I cupped her cheek in one palm and caressed her bottom lip with my thumb. "I'd love it if you stayed the night again."

Jade's eyes smoldered, and she leaned into my hand. "I don't have anything to wear tomorrow," she argued, weakly.

"We can stop by your place to grab a few clothes when I pick you up tonight."

"A *few* clothes?" she asked.

I smiled, making it clear that my words did indeed mean what they implied.

"Okay," she whispered.

I leaned in and kissed her, deeply, hiding none of the feelings she inspired in me. "See you soon, my darling."

"See ya," Jade said, with an oddly shy smile before getting out of the car.

I watched her walk towards the large, high tech building with tall glass windows, her short skirt swaying around her beautiful legs. Only once Jade had entered the building did I turn the car around and allow my seething rage to show. The black car had stopped along the sidewalk, parking three cars from the parking lot's entrance. Although it tried to remain inconspicuous, they couldn't escape my notice now that I'd become aware of them.

I knew who they were but couldn't help wondering what they wanted and why the fuck they would stalk my mate. Driving off the highway to the city outskirts, I pulled into the parking lot of an old, abandoned factory. Parking dead in the center, I got out of the car and stood with my hands clasped behind my back, waiting. The black car slowed down as it approached the building, the driver appearing to hesitate before agreeing to put an end to this charade and turning into the parking lot. The car stopped ten meters from me, two men stepping out of the vehicle.

I immediately recognized the younger of the two men; the same one who'd worn the flat cap at the mall. My hackles raised at the malevolent energy thrumming around him. He had a dark soul. The emotions and desires he broadcast, although unclear to me, had a slimy feel to them. In direct contrast, the driver, a male in his late forties, early fifties, exuded an aura of calm, strength, and honorability that, if not for his companion's toxic presence, would have put me at peace. About six-foot-four, physically fit, dark brown hair with a sprinkle of grey and a clean-shaven square jaw, he epitomized the perfect secret agent, or in this case, Man in Black.

"Greetings, Mistwalker," the older male said, removing his sunglasses, revealing deep blue eyes framed by unexpected smile wrinkles. "I am Agent Thomson, and this is my partner, Agent Wilkins," he added, gesturing towards the younger man.

Wilkins sneered, the contempt—no, more like disgust—on

his face unmistakable. Repressing my anger and the violent sentiments he stirred within me, I focused my attention on Agent Thomson.

"Kazan Dale," I said as introduction. "But then, I'm sure you already knew that."

"Of course, we do, demon," Wilkins spat out.

"Wilkins," Agent Thomson said, the warning unmistakable despite his calm tone.

Wilkins sniffed but kept quiet.

"Why are you stalking me? More importantly, why are you stalking my mate?"

Wilkins snorted then cast his eyes down and clenched his jaw under the hard stare from his senior partner.

"We are trying to understand why you linger here."

Thomson's brutal honesty pleased me. I'd feared he would beat around the bush and play the mental games the authorities seemed to enjoy all too often when dealing with suspects.

"You incarnated in this form two days after the last Mist," Thomson said, gesturing at my human vessel, "and made contact with your woman the day after. That's almost a month ago now. Your kind usually takes their chosen back to the Mist Plane within the 72 hours. But not you. What are your intentions?"

I crossed my arms over my chest and lifted my chin in defiance.

"Why is that any of your concern? I have done no wrong."

"No wrong, my ass!" Agent Wilkins interjected. "There are two human men in a vegetative state who would strongly argue with that statement, if they could, demon."

"I am no demon," I said dismissively. "What makes you think I have anything to do with those men's condition?"

"We have cameras pretty much everywhere in the city since the Mist," Thomson said, matter-of-fact. "We acknowledge the first attack as self-defense, but you coming back to drain them when they were already down doesn't qualify as such."

I shrugged. "They'd drained me. I needed to replenish my reserves so as not to be forced back to the Mist."

"Where you belong," Wilkins said.

We both ignored him.

"Be that as it may," Thomson said in a reasonable tone, "you can't go around draining humans whenever you run low."

"Nor have I," I said, growing tired of this discussion. "I only care about one thing; my Jade. If you've been stalking us as much as I now believe you have, then you'll know we have broken no laws and stirred no trouble. We just want to be left alone and lead a normal life."

"Then take her to your world," Thomson said, his tone halfway between commanding and pleading.

"Jade will not want to leave her sister," I said, running my hand through my hair. "I would love nothing more than to just take her to my realm, but her happiness comes before anything else. If she wishes to spend her human lifespan in the Mortal Plane, I will adapt to this world to be by her side. And when the time of her passing comes, I will take her across the Veil and into the Mist."

Agent Thomson slowly nodded his head, a glint akin to respect in his eyes. "You love her."

It wasn't a question.

"With everything that I am," I said.

Wilkins snorted and rolled his eyes.

"Get back in the car, Wilkins," Thomson said, his voice icy.

"What?" Wilkins asked, outraged.

"Get in the fucking car," Thomson snapped.

I repressed a smile and the urge to shove my fist down the obnoxious jerk's throat. With a huff and a venomous glare in my direction, Agent Wilkins turned on his heels and got back into the car, slamming the door with a bit too much force.

"Forgive him," Thomson said. "He's a rookie and an ex-cop who recently joined the squad. His baby sister 'died' six years ago in one of those Mist Pacts. He refuses to admit she went of her own free will, that she chose a 'demon' over her family."

"Is that how you see us?" I asked. "Demons?"

"Some of you definitely are," Agent Thomson said without aggression or blame in his voice. "And when they are set loose in the population, they wreak serious havoc and bring tragedy to many innocent humans."

I didn't doubt his words. Some of the Mistwalkers were born of nightmares, driven by the single-minded need to hurt and feed off the terror of their victims, leaving dried up husks behind.

"For that idiot and me," he said gesturing with his head at Wilkins inside the car, "it is our job to send those monsters across the Veil and clean up their mess to avoid creating panic among the citizens. Ignorance is bliss."

I nodded slowly. "I am not one of them. You know that I follow your human laws, pay my taxes, and stir no unrest among your people."

"I believe you, which is why we're talking to begin with instead of fighting," he said with a slight smirk. "Note that if you choose to remain in our world, your fake IDs will only take you so far. Anyone who scratches the surface a bit deeper will realize you came into this world, a full grown adult, nine years ago."

I snorted and shook my head. "A situation you could remedy on my behalf, should you choose to," I said with a sliver of sarcasm.

"If I chose to," he confirmed, matter-of-factly.

"Your conditions?" I asked, hooking my thumbs in the back pockets of my pants.

"Keep your nose clean. Keep your woman happy. And above all, no more draining humans." Agent Thomson cast a distracted glance at Agent Wilkins, shifting with visible impatience inside the car. "Don't be a problem for me, and I won't be one for you either."

"Easy enough," I said, keeping my face neutral to hide the

extent of my relief. "But you stay away from my woman," I continued with a sterner tone. "Jade is not a threat to anyone. You and your people will not stalk, harass or intimidate her in any way, shape or form. Any of you have an issue, you come to me. *She* is to be left alone, or *we* will have a problem."

Agent Thomson stared intently at me for a moment and then snorted.

"You've got yourself a deal, Mistwalker."

"Your word," I insisted.

He narrowed his blue eyes at me, a speculative look on his face. "You have my word," he added after a beat. "But break yours, and you will see a very different side of me."

I acknowledged his barely veiled threat with a nod. He returned the gesture then put his sunglasses back on.

"Farewell, Mr. Dale," said Agent Thomson.

"Safe travels, Agent Thomson," I said, watching him turn around and get into his car.

CHAPTER 7
JADE

Three years after I believed my entire life had fallen apart and lost all meaning, I finally realized that I'd never known true happiness until now. Kazan was more than a dream come true. Sure, we still had our little issues to work out, and granted, during the honeymoon phase of a new relationship, things always seemed perfect. But this was different. No man had ever made me feel so loved and worshipped.

In our first couple of weeks together, I feared he might prove not alpha enough with his almost subservient way of trying to please me. I didn't think myself particularly submissive and most certainly didn't want anyone thinking themselves my master. I also had no interest in BDSM aside from the occasional kink play, but I liked dominant men. Kazan had certainly proved that he possessed that trait in the bedroom. The ridiculous number of explosive orgasms he'd given me in the past week still had me reeling... and craving more.

Although I didn't want to trash talk Patrick now that he'd moved on to someone else, I couldn't deny that he'd often been a bit selfish in our intimacy. Kazan never climaxed without making sure I had, and usually at least twice at that. But sex was just the amazing cherry on top. Aside from food, Kazan and I liked so many of the same things. He loved art and excelled at it. He didn't begrudge me the time I spent drawing and painting, getting 'into the zone' as I called it. Instead, he shared it with me as we painted side by side, in harmonious silence, content with the presence of the other. He loved playing video games and would lose graciously to me or win with class against me. We both enjoyed reading, watching nerdy TV shows—mainly of the sci-fi and paranormal type—and hanging out at home in baggy clothes or mostly naked.

With the exhibition planned for the end of next week, we didn't get to go out much, which frankly didn't bother either of us. I loved posing for Kazan, and waiting to see his finished work had me all but climbing the walls. Since we'd become intimate, he no longer asked me to think naughty thoughts to get me in the right headspace and show him a lascivious expression. He would go down on me or flat out make love to me right there on the set, then rush to sketch or paint me while spasms of ecstasy continued to course through me.

Since his first night at my house, things had changed… for the better. While Kazan still bent over backwards to please me, after that first breakfast when I forced him to try multiple variations of coffee, he became more vocal about expressing his preferences when they differed from mine. I loved to see the little quirks that made him unique, not the borderline creepy mirror of myself he had displayed at first.

Although it didn't impede on our happiness, I was more than ever convinced that Kazan suffered from some sort of condition. Not wanting to make him uncomfortable, I didn't bring it up and hoped he'd feel comfortable enough, sooner or later, to confide in me. I no longer thought it to be autism and couldn't find anything through my Internet research that matched his 'symptoms' if they could be called that.

Kazan was an incomplete masterpiece, like someone had

sketched him, done the contour with gradation, and then gave up on coloring with less than 15% left to do. So many things—everyday things—appeared to be new or completely unknown experiences to him. For a gamer, how could he be so clueless about any type of board games? Even non-gamers knew how to play checkers or tic-tac-toe. His knowledge of geography, the political state of the world, and food or fashion trends were less than shallow. Granted, neither of us really watched the news or documentaries, happy to remain in our little bubble, but things seeped in regardless just from living within a society, even just through overheard conversations or magazine covers on newsstands.

That made me wonder if maybe he suffered from some kind of memory disorder, but even that didn't work because, aside from general things people normally knew, he didn't show any inability to remember anything we discussed or did; quite the opposite. Asking Laura about it would have been great, but I didn't want my sister to think my boyfriend mentally impaired before they had a chance to meet.

It confused me but didn't actually concern me.

My phone beeped with the sound of a notification. Peering at it made me smile.

"I miss you."

My Kazan…

I replied that I missed him, too. My chest tightened as I glanced up at the closed shutters in my living room. In a few minutes, the City Defense Alarm would go off. For the hundredth time, I kicked myself for declining Kazan's offer for me to spend the next Mist at his house, or for him to spend it at mine. My insistence on staying home alone during those three days had confused the heck out of him. Coming up with a valid excuse had been a struggle, and I'd failed miserably.

When I told Kazan he needed the quiet time to finish the collection, he'd argued that my presence wouldn't stop him from working, as proven by the past week. I countered that he'd have been even further along without our countless naughtier distractions, which he couldn't argue. When that didn't convince him, I claimed to have lots of work, which required concentration as well. That wasn't actually a lie. Over the years, I'd seized the three days of the Mist as an opportunity to catch up on my work, be it professional or personal.

But work had nothing to do with it.

This would be my first Mist since the Mistwalker had entered my life. I needed to set the record straight with him and didn't want to risk Kazan witnessing any of it. Since the fog had lifted, the Mistwalker had not visited me at night, although he'd been present every time Kazan and I made love. If my instincts proved right, he had entered into some kind of a deal with my boyfriend, and I needed to understand what that meant for us as a couple.

I'd followed Kazan's directive to focus on him, think only of him during our intimate moments. It had been a little challenging the first time, but now, although I couldn't simply block out the Mistwalker, since I felt his presence so strongly, he'd become some kind of extension of my lover, an intrinsic part of him. Still, some sliver of guilt lingered. Despite Kazan's apparent blessing, I still didn't feel comfortable in what I perceived as a threesome. No matter how much monster porn turned me on, I wanted to belong to a single man and him to me.

A few minutes after 8:00 PM, the wail of the siren rose outside. Being a creature of habit, I instinctively rose to my feet and did the round again to make sure every access to the house had been secured. As a proper night owl, I rarely went to bed before midnight—although 1:00 AM qualified more as the standard. Tonight, however, I had a date with a monster. After turning off all the lights, I climbed the stairs to my bedroom, my pulse increasing with each step. Slipping out of one of my many oversized shirts, I rummaged through my sleepwear drawer, shocked to find it mostly empty.

It shouldn't have surprised me though. Over the past week, more and more of my clothes and personal items had made their way to Kazan's flat, while a non-negligible amount of his own wardrobe had found its way into mine. When he gave me a set of his house keys, Kazan had hinted in the least subtle of ways that he'd like me to move in with him. Even though my head said it was too early, too soon, it felt right. But not until this whole mess with the Mistwalker had been resolved. If all went well, I would surprise him by accepting on the night of his exhibit.

Ignoring the two remaining frilly negligees in my drawer, I slipped on a plain, black cotton nightgown. There would be no tempting my Mist demon.

Crawling under the blankets, I sent one last text message to Kazan letting him know I was calling it an early night so he wouldn't worry if he tried to text me again and I failed to answer. Who knew how long it would take to settle things with the Mistwalker.

'Goodnight, my Jade.'

'I'll dream of you.'

And I would, as soon as I'd handled this thing.

'See you in your dreams.'

I responded to his last message with a heart emoji then put the phone on the nightstand. An uneasy feeling settled in the pit of my stomach. Closing my eyes, I began the ever-annoying toss and turn marathon, waiting for the ever elusive sleep.

Time ticked by, minutes, hours, God only knew. As I began turning for the umpteenth time, the most powerful tingling I'd ever felt descended upon my skin. Before my eyes even flicked open, I already knew he'd be inside my room. Rolling onto my back, my breath caught in my throat as the ominous, shadowy wraith-like form of the Mistwalker hovered at the foot of my bed.

"My mate," his disembodied voice said in my head.

Startled, my gaze flicked to my window, perfectly secured

like I'd left it. No Mist swirled around the floor either, indicating that any other door or window might have been breached.

"You cannot be inside my house," I whispered, horrified and yet not fearing for my life. However he got in, he didn't want to harm me and wouldn't allow any of the Mistbeasts to do so either. "It's impossible for you to get in."

I tried to sit up, but a wave of energy pinned me in place. Dark, smoky tendrils, flowed from his shadowy aura, slipping under the blanket and wrapping like vines around my body. His ethereal form glided over the footboard of the bed as he hovered over me, his face stopping inches from mine.

"I can come and go as I please, my Jade. *You* invited me in."

"No! I didn't!" I said, refusing to acknowledge the little voice in my head calling me a liar.

I'm not ready.

A deep part of me knew what I wasn't ready for. Even as the thought crossed my mind, I couldn't quite put into words what I feared, what I'd sheltered myself from under a thick coat of denial. But I knew that facing that truth would destroy the happiness I had found. If closing my eyes and enshrouding myself in flimsy rationalization allowed me to hang on to it, then I didn't want anyone messing with it.

"Time to face the truth, my love," the Mistwalker said, as if he'd just read my mind.

He lowered down into me, his ethereal form passing through my body while a million tiny ice shards stabbed at it. I screamed at the unpleasant—but not painful—sensation then screamed even louder as I seemed to fall out of my body at an incredibly high speed and into an endless void.

"Do not fear, my Jade. As long as I am by your side, no harm will ever come to you."

My stomach lurched as the speed of my descent rapidly decelerated, then came to a halt, with the same queasy sensation one gets on a roller-coaster. Still paralyzed, I watched helplessly as my body straightened into a vertical position before landing, light as a feather, on a dark grey surface. My feet slightly sank into the unfamiliar, cushion-like terrain. Delimited by a wall of Mist, a wide and empty circular area surrounded us, reminding me of a circus ring.

The Mistwalker glided out of my body, leaving me with a strange sense of loss. He turned around to face me, his glowing, yellow eyes hypnotizing me.

"Why did you bring me here?" I blurted out without thinking.

"Because you wanted me to," he said calmly.

"No, I didn't!"

"Would you prefer we have this conversation in your house?"

Although featureless, his eyes, combined with the mocking tone in his voice, made my face heat. I hated stupid people, but even worse were those who merely feigned stupidity. I'd been doing plenty of that in the past few weeks as a coping mechanism.

"What is this place?" I asked to shift the topic. "Who are you? What do you want?"

The Mistwalker glided around me, like a predator circling its prey. I could move, yet remained rooted, only turning my head to keep an eye on him over my shoulder.

"This is the Mist Plane, where dreams are born and come to die." His wistful tone stirred something strange within me. "The place where everything is possible if you wish it hard enough."

He circled back and stopped in front of me, barely three feet between us.

"You know perfectly well who I am, Jade. I am your greatest Wish, and I want you to be my mate for eternity."

His words, his proximity, and the intensity of his gaze unnerved me. I took a step away from him.

"What's my name, Jade?"

The yellow glow in his eyes shone brighter as he took a step forward.

"I… I don't know," I said, suddenly out of breath, then took a couple more steps back.

"Yes, you do. Say my name, Jade. Say it!"

"I don't know. I don't know," I said in a loop, moving away as he continued to advance on me.

Out of the corner of my eye, I could see the wall of Mist looming nearby. Casting a panicked look over my shoulder, I realized that three more steps would put me inside the Mist; a more dire prospect than facing *him*.

"What's my fucking name?" the Mistwalker shouted, his hands grabbing me by the shoulders.

My heart leapt to my throat with the irrational fear that he would shove me into the Mist.

"Kazan!" I screamed, holding on to him, surprised that my hands didn't go through his body. "Kazan… Your name is Kazan," I said in a broken voice as something deep inside me shattered.

He pulled me into his embrace, his ethereal body taking on Kazan's human appearance. Burying my face in the crook of his neck, I bawled my eyes out. Through my broken sobs, I felt his confusion and distress as he caressed my hair in a soothing motion.

"Why such sadness, my Jade? You knew from the first time we met in that supermarket. And yet, you wrapped yourself in a thick shield of denial, even going so far as to imagine you were cheating on me with some demon. Why? You wished me."

What did that even mean?

"I don't understand," I sniffled as more tears poured down my cheeks.

He picked me up in his arms and carried me back to the center of the ring. The scenery around us changed. My throat tightened as I recognized the locker room of Pine Hill High

School where Aunt Clara had sent me after my parents had died. I'd been so miserable there, not only from mourning the still recent loss of my parents, but also from bullying for being such a misfit. I'd just turned thirteen. Joining a new school, halfway through the semester had been bad enough, but worse was doing so while going through that terrible teenage phase where my arms and legs seemed too long for my body, my face kept erupting in pimples, and my nicest clothes were hand-me-downs from my cousin. Being a nerd hadn't helped my cause either. At least I'd never needed braces.

Kazan sat down on one of the benches in the locker room and cradled me on his lap.

"This is the moment of my true birth," Kazan said, looking around the room with wonder. "You might have wished for me before that day, but if you did, they'd all been shallow and passing, which would have made me no more than a spark at the back of your mind." He wiped the tears off my right cheek in a gentle caress. "But that day, you'd been terribly hurt and wished for me harder than you'd ever wished before; hard enough that I became self-aware. You wanted someone who would love you unconditionally, just the way you are, with all your perceived flaws and quirks; someone who would never mock or ridicule you, hurt you, or lie to you. Someone who would be proud to tell the whole world that you were his, and he was yours. You wished me."

A shiver ran down my spine as I remembered that day. Nicolas Merryl had been one of the school's heartthrobs. When he first started showing me some attention, I pushed him away, thinking he was trying to make fun of me. But he didn't relent. For weeks, he hounded me, escalating the intensity of his efforts to sway me until I finally began to believe it. The first time I let him kiss me, he'd dragged me into the girls' locker room during lunch time when everyone else was at the cafeteria. That kiss started out as magical. I had never been kissed before and never imagined my first would come from such a handsome, popular guy.

Things quickly went south, literally, as Nicolas tried to grope me. When I fought him off, he lost his cool, yelling at me that he was done with this fucking bet, to just let him get to third base. I'd punched him and screamed loud enough to make him run away for fear of getting caught. After he left, I sat on the bench, at the same spot where Kazan and I were currently sitting, and cried my broken heart out, wishing for someone just like him.

"After that, we spent a lot of time together," Kazan said wistfully. "You dreamt of me every night. They were nice dreams, sweet dreams, full of innocence and laughter. You wanted a handsome companion who would enjoy just being with you, playing Dungeon & Dragons, holding hands, stealing kisses—no tongue—and taking you to the movies, the park, the beach, etc. It was a lovely time."

I didn't remember those dreams, never remembered any of them in the morning, but yes, I would have wanted all that he'd described.

The scene changed around us, becoming my small room at Uncle William's house after Aunt Clara had deemed she'd done her fair share of caring for the orphans. Having turned sixteen, I'd pleaded with him to let me turn the old storage room in the basement into my personal bedroom. Sharing my room with my then ten-year-old sister, Laura, had long since stopped being cool.

"In the sixteen months leading to that day, you'd been dreaming less and less of me. Having passed that awkward phase, you'd been blossoming into a beautiful young woman and had your first proper boyfriend," Kazan said. "It was a difficult, lonely time for me. I would sit in your high school locker room to dream of you and hope you'd remember me. And then you saw that racy picture of the Beauty and the Beast on an art forum. From that day forward, you dreamt often of me. Instead of the cute teenaged boy you used to picture me as before, you'd dream of me as the Beast ravishing you as Belle, or as a werewolf having his way with you wearing nothing but your red hooded cape, or increasingly, as an alien abducting you before turning you into his very willing sex slave."

My cheeks burned. People would have considered me twisted for all the fantasies I'd entertained at that time. Although I'd been regularly dating guys, I remained a virgin until twenty-one, giving it up to Patrick. Sure, I'd had some heavy petting before that with previous boyfriends, and I'd even given a few blow jobs, but at the time, I'd been seeking my true release in my dreams. While I never remembered the details in the morning, they'd been vivid enough for me to know I'd been naughty in my dreams with something less than human.

Stealing a look up at Kazan, the tenderness in his eyes turned me inside out.

"No, Jade. Patrick didn't claim your virginity; I did. For years, I was your only lover. We learned together. Those nights I brought you here during the last Mist, your head tried to deny us, but your body knew me, recognized us and the rightness of our mating."

Oh God! He is reading my mind.

Kazan smiled.

I shook my head in disbelief. Technically, Patrick had popped my cherry, but this explained why we'd both found me unusually skilled on our first night together. If not for my virginal blood on the sheets, he wouldn't have believed he'd been my first, not that it had been as meaningful for him as it had been for me. Despite the sadness breaking me up inside, it pleased me to know that Kazan claimed first night, even if it had taken place in an illusionary world.

"When you turned eighteen, you began having nightmares about all the things that could go wrong if you went ahead and left your uncle's house and demanded custody of your baby sister. I chased them away and took you to happier places, helping you build your courage so that you could follow your dreams."

I stared at him, speechless. It had been a scary time and yet, I'd felt invincible taking on that challenge. Could a figment of my imagination have built up my confidence in my dreams?

"A year later, nine years ago, your people tore the fabric of the Veil, opening a portal between our worlds. Your aura shone like the brightest beacon, calling me. I raced through the closest portal and straight to you. But you were already locked away," Kazan said, his face taking on a faraway expression. "For three days, I hounded your dreams, begging you to come out into the Mist, to come to me. You refused, saying you couldn't leave your sister. I knew then that if we were ever to be together, I would have to come into your world."

I shuddered, feeling the sudden need to pull away from him. Rising to my feet, I took a few steps forward, but my tiny bedroom didn't offer much room to move about. The room faded, and we found ourselves back in the ring surrounded by a wall of Mist.

"So, what did you do?" I asked, in an accusatory tone. I waved at him, also standing. "Did you steal that poor man's body so that you could get to me?"

"What?" Kazan asked, a disbelieving expression on his face. "I didn't steal anything. This is your wish," he said, indicating his body with a wave of his hands. "You've given me many appearances over the years, but after you began having your alien warrior fantasies, this is the one you always returned to."

The dark shirt and pants he'd been wearing vanished as he stood stark naked before me. I hugged myself, swallowing painfully despite my dry throat.

"This is what you wanted. A giant, with bulging muscles, an angel's face, and a huge cock." Kazan spread his arms wide. "I am as you wished me."

The perfect warrior as dreamed up by a horny teenager who wouldn't think of the inconveniences such a body could represent for a man in the real world. It hadn't mattered because he hadn't been real.

I shook my head, frowning. "It's not possible. My Kazan, the man I've been sleeping with, who has been painting me, driving me to work, and taking me out is real. You're... you're..."

"I AM real," Kazan shouted, slapping his chest with both palms. "In both planes, I. AM. REAL."

Tears pricked my eyes again. Of course, my perfect man would only be an illusion.

"I've seen what happens to Mistwalkers when the Mist goes away. You turn to ash!" I said, angrily wiping tears from my face. "So how are you my Kazan?"

He ran his fingers through his hair, fisting them at the back of his head.

"The human vessel is excruciating to bring into existence. It requires tremendous energy and, without a direct link to our creator, it is difficult to remain anchored. At the end of the first Mist nine years ago, I spent every minute of every day hunting Mistbeasts, Nightmares, and your Wish sparks, absorbing their energy to build my reserves, hoping that the Veil would tear again to allow me through to your realm. And then it did."

My eyes widened. "You hunted my other Wishes?"

Kazan stared back at me, unflinching. "Yes, Wishes and Nightmares alike. I assimilated the good ones to remain your greatest Wish, and fed off of the others."

I swallowed hard, not knowing how to feel about this and unnerved by the predatory glint in Kazan's eyes.

The scene changed around us and turned into an alley, surrounded by buildings in advanced states of disrepair and clearly unfit for habitation.

"This is where I came to take my human form, away from humans and Mist creatures alike. It took me the first day of the

Mist to find this place and almost all of the second day to take my human form." Kazan looked down at himself, frowning, then back up at me. "The human vessel is so fragile and confining. I spent the next day learning to deal with gravity, finding clothes to protect my vessel from the cold, and shoes to shield my feet from pain and injuries."

"But where did you sleep? What did you eat?" I asked, coming to realize how alien it must have been to him.

"I moved to populated areas once the Mist lifted. It was difficult since the Mist is to us like oxygen is to humans. But I adjusted to the vessel and begged for food and money."

The scene shifted again, showing an old shed.

"Knowing I wouldn't last very long, I searched for a safe place to put my money and what clothes or other items I'd managed to acquire. I feared that when my human vessel died, that I would also turn to ash. But the human mind is a natural doorway through the Veil. My vessel went to sleep, and I entered the Mist where I remained while rebuilding twice as much energy."

I pressed a hand to my chest, my mind reeling as I realized the lengths he had gone to reach me.

"But... What happened to your body?" I asked.

"It died," Kazan said with a shrug. "Homeless people die all the time on the street, living under such terrible conditions. No one would question finding the corpse of another nameless one. For that reason, I took on a different appearance each time. Finding the same dead man every other month would have raised too much suspicion. But with my growing wealth of items and money, it got easier each month. It took me three years, but I eventually raised enough to get some IDs made for myself. From that point on, I officially became Kazan Dale, the sketch artist making people's portraits in the park, at the fair, or any other public places I'd be allowed to."

"Until you got noticed and grew famous," I completed. "But

why did you keep disappearing for lengthy periods if you could come back every month?"

"One month of hunting in my realm only gave me enough energy to remain for about one week in the Mortal Plane since building the body drained half of my reserves. Each additional month I hunted gave me an extra week in your world. So, I would hunt for four to six months, sometimes even longer, so that I could stay for significantly more time. It also simplified things for me, as I couldn't allow Kazan Dale to die. Discarding his vessel without alerting people required far more effort and ingenuity."

Feeling dizzy, I looked around for a place to sit. Sensing my need, Kazan shifted our surroundings into Keating Park where he and I often strolled or sat by the pond, talking or sketching. I let myself drop onto the bench, raised my bare feet up, and hugged my knees to my chest. Instead of taking a seat next to me, Kazan willed a shirt and shorts back onto his naked body then kneeled on the grass in front of me before sitting back on his haunches. An early afternoon sun shone down on him, reflecting on the dark waves of his hair, and giving his stunning face an angelic quality.

A terrible thought crossed my mind.

"What have you done with your current body?" I asked.

Kazan smiled. "Don't worry, my Jade. My vessel is safe. I can keep him in stasis for a few days, like I have done with your body."

My shoulders sagged with relief. Despite the conflicting emotions coursing through me, I didn't want anything bad to happen to him, whatever the outcome.

"So, you've been building up to this for the past nine years?" I asked.

He hesitated for a moment. Stupidly, that stung.

"For most of it, yes. By the time I'd been established enough to want to approach you in your world, you'd met Patrick. I kept hoping in vain that it would end. The closer you grew to him, the less you dreamt of me." Upon saying those words, Kazan rubbed his chest as if his heart ached. "For months, I called to you in your dreams without answer. And then, one day you let me in only to say farewell, because you and Patrick were talking of marriage. It nearly broke me, but I wished you well and let you go."

That hurt even more.

"You just let me go? You didn't fight for me?"

It was stupid to let that upset me, but it did. Patrick hadn't fought for us, too eager to return to his ex. My aunts and uncle who looked after us hadn't fought to keep me either when I first talked about leaving. None of my previous boyfriends or simply friends made any extra effort to keep our relationships going when life caused us to see less and less of each other. Was I not worth fighting for?

"I wanted to," Kazan said, clasping his hands on his lap, his knuckles quickly whitening. "In truth, I wanted to kill him for touching what was mine, for taking you from me. For usurping my place by your side…"

His eyes flicked up to mine, hurt and anger burning within. Instead of frightening me, it soothed my sense of rejection.

"Why didn't you?" I whispered.

"Because he made you happy. The sole purpose of my existence has been ensuring your happiness, and you'd found it with him. Interfering for my own selfish needs would have jeopardized that."

"That's when your agent said you were taking an indefinite break," I said, as understanding dawned on me.

Kazan nodded slowly. "I returned to the Mist, and went into some kind of hibernation, waiting for the day when you would need me again, or the day your mortal lifespan ended, to offer you to join me for a second life in the Mist."

My eyes pricked again, and my chest tightened. "You would have waited a lifetime for me?"

"Of course," Kazan said, as if it was obvious. "As long as your light shines, I will be there to help ensure your happiness by any means necessary." His face took on an embarrassed expression. "I'm sorry it took so long for me to realize you were miserable. After Patrick left, your sorrow took a while to reach me through my stasis. It also took time for me to rebuild my strength, a new vessel, and start the collection. I could only make four paintings per month before I had to return to the Mist for five months to rebuild my strength."

My jaw dropped. "Three years…" I whispered. "You've been preparing this collection for the past three years since Patrick left me."

Kazan smiled. "Each painting represents one of your fantasies we experienced together. I finished the last painting two months ago. I had planned on spending five months gorging myself with energy so that I could approach you, at long last, in your world like I did at the supermarket last month. Your sister leaving the window open changed everything."

"How?" I asked, blown away by those revelations. "The part of you that went inside me?"

"Yes. It anchored me to you, allowing me to feed from your emotions. A day by your side is the equivalent of a month of hunting." His eyes smoldered as they roamed over me. I instinctively tightened my arms around my legs still pressed to my chest. "I can feed from your emotions both here and in the Mortal Plane. Those three nights of the last Mist, your pleasure gave me more than enough energy to create a new vessel. My impatience almost ruined everything, though. I was too weak and had to leech from your emotions not to be forced back to the Mist. I should have gorged a bit more before coming to you, but I couldn't wait anymore."

More conflicted than ever, I got up and walked up to the

railing surrounding the small pond in the garden. From the corner of my eyes, I watched Kazan rise to his feet and approach me. He stopped behind me, the heat of his body seeping through the cotton nightgown I still wore—or rather the dream version of it. With great care, Kazan wrapped his arms around me, as if fearing I would balk, then pressed his chest against my back.

Tears pricked my eyes again as I relaxed against him. How many times had we stood exactly like that in this very location on the Mortal Plane in the past month? My life had been so perfect then.

"Why the sadness?" he asked again, confusion in his voice. He turned me around to face him. "There are no more obstacles between us. We can be together forever." His eyes flicked between mine, searching. "You wished me. You wished us. Am I no longer what you want?"

"Oh Kazan," I said, tears falling down my cheeks again as my heart broke for him and for us. "You are so perfect, beyond perfect. I always thought you were too good to be true, but now…"

"I AM true," he said forcefully. "Your wish may have been my spark of life, but I have thrived, I have grown. I am real in both our worlds!"

I nodded and gazed at his beautiful face through blurred vision. Cupping his face in my hands, I let my palm caress a path down his cheeks, his thick neck and broad shoulders before resting on his muscular chest. Kazan closed his eyes under my touch, the expression on his face a mixture of pleasure and despair. He could feel my emotions just like I could feel his, and mine were telling him goodbye.

"Yes, Kazan. You are real in all the ways that matter. And yes, you are perfect, exactly everything I've ever wished for in a man, except for one very important thing; you didn't *choose* me. You may have become real, but this relationship is not."

"How can you say that?" Kazan asked, his face tensing with

anger. His arm tightened its hold behind my back while his right hand held my nape firmly, but not painfully. "I love you! I've loved you from the moment I achieved self-awareness. I have walked two worlds just to be with you, and I will travel a thousand more if I must. Have I not made you happy in the past month? Have I not shown the depth of my feelings for you?"

"Yes, you have, but you had no other choice. You're my Wish. I *programmed* you to love no one else but me, no matter what."

"I'm not a machine," Kazan snapped, letting go of me as if I'd burnt him.

But you might as well be.

I heaved a sigh, trying to figure out how to make him understand. "Love should be freely given, Kazan, not imposed. How can you truly love me when you never chose me?"

He tilted his head to the side and narrowed his eyes. "The same way mortals love their parents and their siblings. You didn't choose Laura, did you? Given a chance, would you exchange her for another?"

Of course not.

"It's not the same though. Family—"

"Love is love," Kazan interrupted. "A puppy doesn't choose its master, but that will not stop it from developing a true and lasting love for him, and vice versa."

"You're not an animal," I said, starting to feel irritated myself.

"No, but I'm a sentient being, like animals or humans, capable of feelings and emotions. Love can blossom in various ways. There is no rule for how it should come to be. That mine for you came in a non-traditional way doesn't make it any less true."

I pursed my lips, slightly annoyed.

"Do you like your body?" I asked.

He blinked, confused by the sudden change of topic. "It is a very nice body," he said, looking at himself. "Any man would be proud to have one such as this."

"It is nice, but that's not what I asked you," I said. "Do you *like* it?"

"Yes," he said, increasingly confused.

"Really?" I challenged. "You enjoy struggling to find clothes of your liking that will fit you, or having to bend your head in the subway because you're too tall, and feeling cramped in most cars because they're not adapted to your height?"

He flinched, his face taking on a troubled expression. "It's a mild inconvenience in the Mortal Plane."

"One that my wish imposed on you."

He shrugged. "So what? Humans don't get to choose their bodies either. The genetics of their parents decide, and they learn to deal with it."

Fair point.

"Okay, I'll give you that one. Let's talk about food then. I bet you and I often had ribs, wings, Sangria and pancakes in our times together while I dreamt, and you loved them. But in my world, you hate them."

He crossed his arms over his chest, looking slightly annoyed. "I don't hate them, but so what if I did? I can eat something else while you continue to enjoy them. The human body's taste buds ruin many things but elevate others. In time, I'll just adapt to the way this vessel changes my perceptions and likes, the same way I adjusted to gravity."

"And *that* is exactly my point," I said, running a nervous hand through my hair. "My world is riddled with physical and biological rules that constrain and define us." I waved at the illusionary park we stood in. "Here, your size doesn't matter. You only need to wish for something you like to fit, and it will. For all I know, in this world, Sangria tasted like a smoked salmon and cream cheese bagel to you. And that's just fine. But in my world, you cannot wish unpleasant things to fit in with something more agreeable or palatable. You have to accept them the way they are or move on."

I reached for his hands and held them in mine.

"I do love you, Kazan but, in my world, you are incomplete. Most of those things are superficial, like food, which I would love to help you explore and discover. Others are far more profound, and as you discover them, you might realize that I'm not the love of your life."

Kazan opened his mouth to argue, but I released one of his hands to place my fingertips on his lips.

"I want you to love me for who I am, with all my quirks, especially the ones that cannot be wished away. And I want to love you for who you are, not who you think you must be to make me happy. But above all, I want you to be happy with who you are and to be yourself, by choice. Do you really want to be an artist? Do you really want to be a nerdy Star Trek and D&D fan? Who is the real Kazan?"

Kazan stared at me intently. The hurt and desperation that emanated from him since the start of this conversation faded abruptly. An air of strength and determination descended upon him as he pushed his shoulders back. My stomach knotted as his gaze upon me lost all warmth. Something had changed, and I'd caused it.

"Since you refuse to abandon your sister, if we are to be together, I must come live in the Mortal Plane. However, you believe that the more I stay in your world, the more my person-ality and feelings for you will change. You think it inevitable that sooner or later, I'll leave you for another as I become more 'complete' and see all the 'more suitable' choices that are open to me."

My throat too constricted to speak, I nodded at his perfect summary of my deepest fears.

"Hmmm," he said before looking away, lost in thought.

I shifted on my feet, my sense of unease growing exponentially. Until moments ago, I hadn't realized how I'd been basking in constant waves of love and tenderness from Kazan. But now that he'd shut himself off from me, I felt cold, deprived of his affection cocooning me. Had I wished his feelings for me to die off?

His grey eyes turned back towards me, cold and ominous. I swallowed painfully, waiting for his next words, which I knew would hurt me somehow.

"You have opened my eyes, Jade. I thank you." With a dismissive gesture of his hand, Kazan waved away the park scenery, leaving us back in the empty ring surrounded by Mist. "I will return you to your world now and reflect upon your words. You are right. I'd been so single-minded in my obsession with making you happy that I never considered my own desires and aspirations or even realized that I had choices."

My stomach dropped.

I pushed him away, and now I'm truly losing him.

"Before you go," Kazan added, "I would like you to do some reflecting of your own."

I raised an inquisitive eyebrow.

"When you first met me and thought me human, you took a chance on a handsome stranger, whose relative fame guaranteed he had plenty of sexy women, fans of his work, who could try to steal him from you. A man who, like Patrick, probably had a history of previous girlfriends who might resurface. But I, a man created for you, *by* you, you are ready to discard at the slightest possibility that my feelings for you might change in a hypothetical future. You want a man who will fight to keep you. Shouldn't you be willing to do the same for him?"

I stared at him, words failing me. Kazan didn't give me a chance to respond, not that I knew what to say. He turned around and walked into the Mist.

The floor vanished. As the void swallowed me, my stomach churned with the nauseating sensation of falling. I landed back in my body, feeling dizzy and disoriented. But my physical discomfort represented the least of my worries. My heart ached, lacerated by a thousand claws. In my fear of losing Kazan, I'd been the architect of my own destruction. Why indeed didn't I fight for him? Why had I been so hell-bent on convincing him that our relationship was doomed?

"What have I done?" I whispered.

CHAPTER 8
KAZAN

The Mist parted before me, revealing the dream home I had built for Jade over the years, waiting for the moment we would be together at last. I hadn't set foot back here since Jade and Patrick had started talking about marriage. It had hurt too much. And when they broke up, I'd been too busy building a life in the Mortal Plane to worry about this.

Jade's words had cut deeply. I understood her fears and even admitted they held some merit. But she'd wished me for so many years, it never crossed my mind that her feelings might be so shallow she wouldn't even try to fight for us.

The past nine years had been fraught with challenges. Yet, not once had I wavered in pursuing my course of action, wrapped in my self-righteous conviction that she needed me and that only I could truly make her happy. My entire self-perception had been steeled in the belief that I was her greatest Wish. Over the years, I stalked each new Wish she'd formed, watching their spark flicker and die. If they were good, the rare few who endured and thrived, I absorbed within me before they could become self-aware to remain her greatest Wish. If they were bad, I destroyed them to keep them from festering and tainting her wishing well and absorbed their life force to fuel my own strength.

But as I stood before the massive mansion, my chest burned as if the blood pumping through my heart had turned to acid. The house was garish and poorly conceived; the whimsical creation of a child that would qualify more as a Chimera. She'd been fourteen when she'd first started speaking of her dream house. It reflected each phase of her challenging teenage years, from the gothic wing of the mansion with its dark stone tower and spires, to the futuristic, asymmetrical wing all made of glass with a solar panel dome. In the back, a massive pool boasted a replica of Versailles' Apollo Fountain smack in the middle, eating most of the swimming space. Placing it against one of the edges would have made more sense.

The inside proved to be just as outlandish with a mish-mash of styles and colors, like someone couldn't make up their mind and just went for everything. Today's Jade would hate this place. As much as it broke my heart, she'd been right. All these years, I had fought to have with her the utopian life of the dream world. But with each passing hour, day, week, and month, my life companion had gone from an awkward teenager to a beautiful, strong woman. Through her wishes and dreams, I received glimpses of that evolution, but I didn't truly know her... the real Jade.

My visit to her house in the Mortal Plane had been an eye opener, flipping on their head so many of my beliefs about her and what made her tick. Peaceful and cozy, it held an understated elegance, by no means presumptuous, and with a quirky edge that made it fun and inviting.

I loved her place.

But I loved my own place as well. It dawned on me that my flat had been the first thing I had truly created for myself, according to my own tastes and wishes, without any external influence—at least, no conscious ones. Getting Jade's blessing to browse the bohemian style clothes at Shay & Vincent instead of the biker fashion she preferred had been so exciting.

In the Mortal Plane, I had discovered the meaning of personal likes and dislikes. I wasn't Jade's clone. I was Kazan Dale, an individual with his own preferences and aspirations. In the Mortal Plane, endless possibilities presented themselves to me with a lifetime to explore them. Although terrifying, the prospect of embarking on that journey of self-discovery exhilarated me. Given a choice, would I have picked Jade for a life mate?

Only time would tell if I ended up with her by my side or on a completely different path.

CHAPTER 9
JADE

C *areful what you wish for.*

The sickening thought replayed endlessly through my mind for what proved to be the longest, most miserable Mist of my life. I called out to Kazan, wishing for him to come back or bring me to his world again but was met only with complete silence. I even blew up his phone, calling and texting him in the silly hope he would have returned to his human body.

Nothing.

The three endless days of the Mist gave me far more time than I wanted to reflect not only on the parting question Kazan had asked me before sending me away, but also on why I had handled our relationship the way I had since day one.

Patrick leaving me had hurt terribly, but the past month had shown me what true love with the right partner felt like. Although he'd been a good man, Patrick had not been the one for me. He'd been my first—in the physical world—which I'm sure played a big role in this. After nearly five years together, habit, the comfort of familiarity, and the need for stability convinced me to see things that simply weren't there. In truth, we didn't have a whole lot in common, aside from an easy friendship, dislike of cheaters, and mutual respect. Patrick loved to party it up, I liked staying at home. He needed his regular sports fix, I needed art. He enjoyed action and war movies with shallow storyline but crazy VFX, I loved complex psychological thrillers and sci-fi.

Because of the deep trust between us, I didn't mind him going out with his friends while I did my introvert stuff. In retrospect, we hadn't been as much a couple as friends with benefits.

With Kazan, we'd been on the same wavelength. Yes, I'd wished him that way, but the things that hadn't worked for him, I'd quickly noticed, and they'd been superficial. Kazan hadn't chosen to be an artist, but his passion for it couldn't be denied. I would have loved him even had he preferred a different career. It simply brought us even closer. He understood and lived art the same way I did, but with far more skill.

His innocence and incompleteness helped me look at the world around me with new eyes. I wanted to embark on that journey with him, even if it ended up leading him away from me. Thinking back on when he'd reminisced on how he came to be, the events of my past that had brought him to life, I realized that I wanted to form new memories with him, this time moored in reality and memories that would remain with me forever instead of fading away with the morning light.

I'm going to fight for you, Kazan. I will fight for us. Just, please, let me.

Drawing strength from that new resolve, I tried calling Kazan again but without success. I wouldn't let him ignore me. Although I usually slept in on the post-Mist holiday, I jumped out of bed at 7:00 AM. The City Defense Alarm had gone off half an hour ago. After a quick shower, I got dressed and went through the process of unlocking the house. As per my usual routine, I opened the curtains and shutters in all the rooms upstairs before heading downstairs, starting with my office in the back, then the kitchen, leaving the living room and foyer for last.

After opening the pair of windows on the right side of the kitchen, welcoming in the bright rays of the sun, I went for the patio door. As the shutters began to rise, my heart leapt in my chest as it revealed the prone form of a naked man, leaning against the glass door.

"Oh God!"

I didn't wait for the electric shutters to finish winding up. As soon as they cleared the handle of the door, I unlocked it and slid it open. At first, I believed him to be Kazan seeing how the man, tall and muscular, also had long black hair covering his face. However, the minute the door opened, the tingle that washed over me indicating a Mistwalker's presence didn't belong to my boyfriend. It struck me hard, making my knees wobble and my stomach roil.

The man lifted his head, a handsome, oddly familiar face with striking blue eyes staring back at me. The spark of recognition lit up his features, and his full lips stretched in a victorious smile.

"My Jade," he whispered, his voice hoarse, no doubt from exposure through the night and the chilly morning air.

I recoiled, my sense of unease jumping up a notch. Where I'd felt instant attraction to Kazan, this man oozed danger and far more complications than I could handle right now. But he needed help. He'd die if he remained outside much longer. His skin was an alarmingly pale color, his lips having taken on a slightly blue tinge.

"Can you get up?" I asked, knowing I would never be able to carry someone as tall and massive as he.

Of course, I would have dreamt him as a muscular giant as well.

The Mistwalker growled his assent and leaned heavily on the door frame to get up on his feet. I averted my eyes at the first glimpse of the massive cock dangling limply between his muscular thighs.

"Come in," I said. "I'll be right back."

I ran into the living room to grab the throw blanket from the couch and ran back to the kitchen to find the man stumbling in towards the dining table. He gratefully accepted the blanket I'd extended to him, wrapping it around his imposing body before collapsing to a chair.

"You must be hungry and thirsty," I said, closing the patio door then scrambling towards the kitchen counter. "Let me prepare you something to eat."

"Yes," the man mumbled, nodding his head sluggishly, a famished look in his eyes.

Thinking of things Kazan liked—and hoping the stranger would as well—I pulled out a full pack of bacon and tossed them in a pan then popped some bread into the toaster. Frazzled, my mind raced in every direction. Thankfully, my ability to go into autopilot when life threw me curve balls kicked into action.

The stranger guzzled down the glass of water I'd poured him from the bottled water stash I now kept for Kazan. The man didn't even pause to breathe. I thought of telling him to slow down so as not to make himself sick but stared instead, tongue tied. The popping sound of the toaster reminded me of my current task.

"So... what's your name?" I asked the stranger while turning the bacon in the pan and setting some water to boil to make him tea. Kazan preferred it to coffee, and making a latte for the stranger would take too long.

"Morgan," he said, offering no more.

"How long were you out there?" I asked, quickly assembling a BLT sandwich for him with only a dab of mayo, remembering how Kazan found it sickening when spread too thick.

Instead of a tea, I poured some chicken broth into the boiling water, figuring a clear 'soup' would serve him better.

"Two days," Morgan answered, before timidly bringing the cup of broth to his lips.

"Careful, it's hot," I said, instinctively, still digesting his answer.

He took a sip, wrinkled his nose, and then frowned at the cup.

He doesn't like it.

Still, he wrapped his hands around the warm cup and forced himself to down the whole thing. Unlike Kazan who'd often forced himself to consume things he didn't like to please me, my gut told me Morgan only drank it for the warmth. After two nights naked on my patio, he must have been chilled to the bone.

"How did you survive two days without food or clothes?" I asked, bewildered.

Morgan leveled his steely blue eyes on me, a hard glint shining within. "I fed off of the Walkers and Beasts stupid enough to come within my grasp."

And he'd enjoyed it, too.

A shiver ran down my spine. Unable to sustain his stare, I welcomed him lowering his gaze to his sandwich as he picked up the first half and took a small bite. His eyes widened as he chewed slowly, exploring the complex flavor on his taste buds.

"This is not bad," he said in a pleasantly surprised tone.

Relieved, I turned to the counter to prepare one for myself and a second sandwich for him in case he'd want more. He devoured the first one in a blink, forcing me to rush to finish the next one.

"Yes," Morgan said with a satisfied purr. "This will work nicely to feed this vessel when you can't."

My hand froze halfway through cutting the sandwich, and my eyes flicked towards him.

"Excuse me?" I asked, wanting to believe I'd misheard him.

"This is good, but nowhere near as tasty and filling as you."

Mind racing, hand fisted around my cutting knife, I stared at him, speechless. A sudden pulling sensation made me dizzy. I recognized it as the same energy drain I'd experienced with Kazan before he made a swift exit at the supermarket.

"You're feeding from me," I whispered, horrified. "You're feeding from my emotions!"

"Yes," he said, his face taking on a predatory look. "Be grateful I settle for them instead of your life force."

My anxiety level skyrocketed. Clinging to the knife, I took a step away from him. He rose to his feet, the ends of the blanket hanging open, giving me a full-frontal view of his nudity.

"I want you to stop," I said, taking another step backward, "and I want you to leave."

His temper abruptly flaring, he gave me an angry sneer. "Stop and go away. Even here, you sing the same tired old tune. Always pushing me away. And yet, how eagerly you've spread your legs for the Hunter. You've let him fuck you in the guise of a plethora of monsters, begging for more like a little slut, feeding all the power to him so he'd be strong enough to hunt the rest of us."

"I wished him! I'd never wish the likes of you," I said glancing around me for the best chance to run. And then it dawned on me. "You're a Nightmare!"

His beautiful face twisted, his maw forming an evil rictus. "I am your oldest dream, the sum of all your fears, you cock-teasing bitch. You've barely fed me enough through the years to sustain me, taunting me and making me chase you through dark alleys and abandoned woods. You'd let me break through your flimsy shelters only to deny me at the last minute by escaping the dream, taking away my prize. But *him*," he spat out with contempt, "you let him fuck you as a beast, taking his monstrous cock on all fours like an animal. I'm going to make you *my* bitch, now Jade. You were mine first!"

Morgan slapped his chest on those last words and took a wobbly step towards me.

Gravity! He hasn't adapted to this world yet.

With him standing in the way, I couldn't make a swift exit through the patio door. The front door was still shuttered. Even if he lumbered behind me, I'd never have time to raise the shutters, unlock the door, and get out before he reached me. Despite his current weakened state, I wouldn't make the mistake of underestimating the strength of those bulging arms. The panic room would be faster to handle than the front door but would still require some time to open, get in, and lock up. If I miscalculated and he caught up to me before I'd secured the room, I would effectively turn myself into the stupid horror B movie heroine that ran into the attic with no way out and the murderer hot on her trail. The patio first, or the panic room as backup, represented my best chance of getting away from him.

"Your Hunter's a clever bastard, but so am I. It was ballsy of him to cross over to your plane. But I watched, observed, and learned. He's taken everything from me, now I will take back what's rightfully mine. You will feed me with your terror and your pain."

The pulling sensation tugged harder at me, and my vision blurred for a moment. Morgan hissed, his face dissolving into an expression of pure ecstasy.

"Your fear tastes so damn good. It makes me so fucking hard." Morgan grabbed his fully erect cock and stroked it slowly, holding it so tightly it had to hurt him. "Kazan is a fool for not binding you in all this time. His hold on you is weak. I will fill you to the brim with my seed and my essence. You will never anchor another but me."

He advanced towards me, his steps already steadier. I was weakening quickly while he visibly strengthened by the minute, his skin having already gained a healthy tinge. If I didn't act soon, I'd be too drained to fight back.

"Stand back," I said, slashing the knife at him.

He chuckled, advancing again, still stroking himself. If I could lure him around the table, I could make a dash for the patio door. I'd pushed it closed after giving Morgan the blanket, but I hadn't locked it. Even if he caught me, I'd have time to scream loud enough to alert the neighbors.

As if he'd read my thoughts, he grabbed the two chairs closest to him and tossed them in front of the patio door. While it would be no problem getting them out of the way, the delay would suffice for him to grab me. I needed to create a diversion.

Before I could think of one, Morgan lunged for me. On instinct, I slashed at him with the knife while backing away. My blade made contact. A long, deep gash appeared the length of his forearm. He screamed in agony and fell to one knee. Clutching his right arm to his chest, he stared at it with the horrified expression of someone who'd just had his hand severed.

His excessive reaction confused me for half a beat, and then I realized that aside from cold, thirst, and hunger following his 'birth' in my world, he'd never felt real physical pain. This had to be mind-numbingly excruciating for him. But I didn't give a shit about his pain. This was my opportunity. I made a dash for the patio door. As he still stood in my way, I had to circle around the table to get to it.

"NO!" Morgan shouted.

Still half kneeling, he pushed the table to block my path with his good hand. The heavy wooden table all but flew at me. I screamed and barely managed to dodge out of the way before it crashed into the wall, punching a huge hole in it. His glass and plate fell off the table upon impact, shattering on the floor. Had I not managed to stop, the table would have smashed me into the wall instead. Judging by the damage, I'd have suffered some serious fractures, if not worse.

His strength was even greater than I'd feared.

As Morgan began to rise, his face contorted with pain, something clicked in my mind. Without thinking, I grabbed the glass fruit bowl on the table, threw the fruits at his face before smashing the bowl at his bare feet. He hissed as glass shards stabbed at him. He backed away, stepping on a shard and howled in pain. Rushing to the small kitchen console a few feet away, I picked up the decorative vases and plates adorning it and smashed them in a wider radius in front of him.

"I'm going to make you bleed!" Morgan roared as he pulled out the piece of glass from the sole of his foot.

Heart pounding, I ignored his threat and gathered as many more breakable items as I could manage without cutting myself with the knife. While Morgan tried to figure out a path through the debris, I made a beeline for the panic room, throwing the fragile items to the floor along the way. My fingers shook as I opened the trap door and the sliding metal plate.

His screams of pain and rage had me in a complete state of panic. Hearing all the thrashing behind me, I looked over my shoulder, but he'd still not made it out of the kitchen. A broken sob of relief escaped me as I started down the stairs with no signs of him barreling down on me. I closed the sliding metal plate and activated the switch that would automatically reset the camouflaging wooden boards above it, and then shut all access to my hiding place with the reinforced titanium plate. Even with his strength, Morgan would never get to me here.

Shaking, I fumbled through my pocket to fish out my phone as I stumbled to the couch. My body all but collapsed onto it. Morgan kept screaming upstairs, but the muffled sound prevented me from making out his words.

"Please, please answer," I said while calling Kazan.

His voicemail answered.

Swallowing back more tears, I dialed 911. To my relief, an operator answered rapidly. Since the Mist, emergency personnel was tripled on the day it ended to meet the needs of the population, from missing persons to ashy remains of Mist beings.

"911, what is your emergency?" the female dispatcher asked.

"There's a man in my house trying to hurt me," I said in a trembling voice. "I found him naked outside my patio door while doing my post-Mist unlock. I let him in, thinking he needed help, but as soon as he ate, he turned crazy on me."

"Are you in a safe location right now?"

"Yes. I'm locked inside my panic room," I said, trying to get my pulse and breathing to settle down.

"What is your address?"

"2048 Oak Ridge. The shutters are still down on the front door. The patio door is closed but unlocked."

"Please hold one moment. Don't hang up, okay?"

"Okay."

Holding my breath, I listened for any noise upstairs. Morgan had stopped yelling but the slight thud of his footsteps told me he was hunting for me. Even though I didn't believe him capable of breaking through the titanium plate, I hoped he wouldn't discover the hidden trapdoor.

"Okay, ma'am," the dispatcher said, startling me. "I've got units on their way. They'll be there in less than two minutes."

"Thank you," I said, weeping with relief. "He's very strong, but he's injured. I slashed his arm with a knife, and then I threw glass on the floor to keep him from chasing after me. He's barefoot."

"You did well, ma'am. Can you describe the suspect?"

I did, giving as many details as possible except for him being a Mistwalker. Until Kazan, I'd never heard of one taking on a human form. If I mentioned any of this, she might think me crazy or assume this to be a prank call.

"Stay with me, okay? I'm in direct communication with the agents. Do not open the door to your panic room until I've confirmed with you that the house is secured and that the agents are the ones asking you to open, all right?"

"Yes, ma'am."

When two minutes turned to five, then ten, I asked her what was happening. I couldn't hear Morgan upstairs anymore. In fact, I couldn't hear anyone. She told me they needed to secure the perimeter first, which naturally made sense. Ten more minutes went by before she told me to open the hatch.

My hands shook as I unlocked and opened my only defense. The serious face of an older man, with light grey in his dark brown hair and gentle, deep blue eyes, had me thanking whatever higher power had protected me.

He extended a hand towards me to help me up, and I hung up with the dispatcher. As I stepped onto the landing, I realized he wasn't wearing a police uniform.

"You're not a cop!" I said, my worried gaze flicking towards his companion, busy opening the shutters. He looked at me over his shoulder, and my stomach dropped as I recognized the man who had been stalking me at the mall. "You," I whispered, horrified.

I took a step away from the older man.

"Do not be afraid, Ms. Eastwood," he said, raising his palm in an appeasing gesture. "I'm Agent Thomson, from the Fourth Division. We handle cases like yours, not the cops."

"The Men in Black?" I whispered, flabbergasted. My eyes flicked back to the younger agent. "You've been stalking me."

"Not exactly," Agent Thomson said. "But Mr. Dale's arrival required us to investigate his intentions and assess whether or not he was the same kind of unpleasant visitor you received this morning."

I felt my blood drain from my face and hugged my midsection. They knew about Kazan. What else did they know? What did that mean for us?

"Please, Ms. Eastwood," Agent Thomson said, gesturing towards the living room. "Let's have a seat to discuss the situation."

"Did you find him?" I asked, advancing with hesitant steps, looking at the wreckage Morgan had turned my house into.

"Unfortunately, he escaped," Thomson said, then waved a

hand towards the younger Agent. "Ms. Eastwood, this is my partner, Agent Wilkins."

I distractedly nodded at him, my mind still stuck on Morgan. "How is that even possible," I asked, taking my usual seat in the lazy boy. "He's naked and injured! Surely someone saw where he went? Or at the very least, he left a trail of blood."

"You'd think so," Agent Wilkins said in a sarcastic tone that immediately had my hackles rising. "Except, the blood trail ends in your bedroom, where he found plenty of male clothes to pick from."

My instant dislike of Agent Wilkins grew further. I chose to ignore him and turned to Agent Thomson.

"But I could hear him upstairs, minutes before you arrived. He couldn't possibly have gone far. I gave the dispatcher his description."

"Yes, but considering his nature and his powers, we need specially trained agents to go after him."

"Powers?" I asked, playing dumb.

Just how much do they know?

Agent Thomson's blue eyes took on a harder edge, losing any warmth. "Let's not play games, Ms. Eastwood. You witnessed your boyfriend's powers when those thugs attacked you." He raised his hand to stop me when I opened my mouth to argue. "Do not worry, neither you nor he are in trouble for it. As long as he continues to abide by our laws and not harm humans, Mr. Dale has nothing to fear from us. That other man, though…"

"Morgan," I whispered. "He called himself Morgan."

"How human," Agent Wilkins said, taking a seat close to his partner. "Except that demon isn't human at all. Those Mist-walkers…"

Agent Thomson gave Wilkins a warning glance which shut him up and made me wonder what else the younger agent had intended to say.

The men spent the next half hour giving me the third degree

about Morgan and asking prying questions about my relationship with Kazan, being particularly curious as to why he hadn't spent the Mist with me. I danced around my answers, keeping them as succinct as possible.

"Look, you're here to investigate Morgan, not to pry into my *private* relationship with Mr. Dale," I snapped when Agent Wilkins asked one invasive question too many. "So, unless you can justify to me how this highly inappropriate line of questioning is relevant to finding Morgan, I would ask you to cut it out and get back on topic."

Wilkins pinched his lips, his brown eyes burning with resentment. Thomson smirked, amused by my irritation.

"No, Ms. Eastwood, that will be all," the older man said, rising to his feet.

Wilkins and I followed suit.

"Until we've located the Nightmare," Agent Thomson said, "I highly recommend that you stay with Mr. Dale, preferably at his place. You have verbally welcomed Morgan into your home. Until you've properly rescinded it, he will try to come and go as he pleases. Stick to public places, and avoid being alone at night. He will not stop until he gets to you or we've disposed of him."

I nodded, a cold shiver coursing through me. "I was planning on going to Mr. Dale's house right after breakfast."

"Excellent idea," Thomson said with an approving nod. We both ignored Wilkins' derisive snort. "If you wish, we can stay with you while you gather what you need and walk you out."

I gave him a grateful smile and ran upstairs to pack an overnight bag, not that I really needed anything with so many of my belongings already at Kazan's place. After calling a cab, I verified that all the windows were closed and the patio door locked before exiting, flanked by the two agents.

The security guard at the entrance of Kazan's building nodded in greeting as I made my way to the elevators. One hand clutching my bag, the other fiddling nervously with the set of keys Kazan had given me, I kept wondering what kind of welcome he would grant me. Was he even home? Would he kick me out?

No. Not with Morgan on the loose.

Whatever the state of our relationship, Kazan wouldn't leave me to fend for myself, especially not against a Nightmare. Exiting the elevator, I walked up to his door and rang the doorbell. If he was home, I wanted to give him a chance to choose whether or not to let me in. Leaning forward, I strained my ear but didn't hear any movement. After slipping the key into the keyhole, I was almost surprised that it still worked. No sooner did that silly thought cross my mind than I kicked myself for it.

I pushed the door open. Bright morning light flooded the otherwise empty loft. Since the building had an automated lock-down system, the shutters being open didn't mean Kazan had been around. I called out his name, my voice sounding overly loud in the heavy silence. Taking in a deep, fortifying breath, I headed towards his bedroom, knocked, and then opened the door when he failed to respond.

My heart leapt when I saw Kazan's naked form lying on the bed. His stillness and unnaturally pale skin had me running to his side in panic.

"Kazan! Baby, speak to me!" I said, touching his overly cool skin.

For a moment, I thought he'd stopped breathing, the rise and fall of his chest so subtle I almost missed it. Pressing my head against his chest, the slow but regular beating of his heart reassured me he still lived.

Stasis. Kazan said he'd left his vessel in stasis.

Tears of relief pricked my eyes. My entire body began to

shake as the stress of the Mist, our fight, his absence, and this morning's attack finally got to me. I'd been running on adrenaline and was now crashing hard. Kicking my shoes off, I curled up against Kazan and cried out all the ugliness that had been festering inside of me.

It was liberating.

God, I've become such a cry baby.

I needed to get a grip and get my shit together. I missed the strong woman who'd taken on the responsibility of raising her baby sister at the age of eighteen, defied the naysayers by buying her own house before the age of twenty-six, and got her sister to attend college. I was a go getter, not a pushover. If Morgan hadn't managed to defeat me, nothing and no one else would, least of all my own insecurities.

Lifting my head, I kissed Kazan's cold lips and got up to fetch a washcloth and clean water to wash him. I wanted to believe he'd come back to me soon, but until he did, I'd look after him like he had me for years. To my chagrin, he remained still throughout the bath.

Once done, I walked out of the room and into the studio. The initial set of twenty-four paintings on the display stands drew me. I stopped before each one, looking at them with new eyes. My last visit into the Mist had jogged long lost memories. As I gazed upon them, fragments of recollection flashed through my mind; partial scenes, sounds, even the feel of Kazan's arms around me. Yes, the paintings had moved me so deeply because they were not just dreamed up fantasies, but Kazan's and my history. These were true moments we had spent together in another realm. They weren't wet dreams to him, but his life. Our life together.

I padded over to the work area where the six paintings of me rested on their respective easels facing each other, three on each side. Rooted in place, my gaze roamed over them as I pondered whether or not to approach further since I couldn't properly see them from this angle. However, it felt wrong and disrespectful to proceed without Kazan's blessing. Shoulders drooping, I sighed heavily and looked out the window at the bay, knowing I would respect his wishes.

As I began to turn to leave, I felt him before seeing him, the familiar tingle washing over me. Spinning around, I found Kazan standing in the doorway of the studio, wrapped in a black bathrobe and staring at me with an unreadable expression. My pulse sped up and my throat tightened as he walked into the room, his gait graceful, and stopped a couple of meters away from me, right past the last painting on the display stands.

How could I have pushed him away?

"You came back," I whispered, resisting the urge to run and throw myself into his arms.

"You doubted it?" he asked, raising an eyebrow.

I shrugged then hugged my midsection. "No, not really since you have the upcoming exhibit, but I didn't know when you would."

"Ah... Is that why I smell of soap? Was I already growing rancid?" Kazan asked in a semi-serious tone that I couldn't quite interpret.

My cheeks burned. "No, not at all!" I said, shaking my head, embarrassed. Granted, he hadn't bathed in three days, but he hadn't smelled bad, probably thanks to the stasis. But I wouldn't admit to him that I'd left tear streaks all over him. "I just wanted to look after you until you came around."

He stared at me for a second then looked over his shoulder at the collection. "So, these are the only reason you knew I'd come back?"

My heart leapt as I carefully chose my words, wanting to believe he was giving me an opening to patch things up.

"I *knew* you would return because you're too respectful to let Monica down after all the work she's done preparing your exhibition. I also didn't think you'd leave your body to die here. All your wealth would be seized by the county and the day you wished to return, you'd have to start from scratch again." Kazan frowned, the creases deepening with each of my words. Suddenly feeling coy, I tucked my hair behind my ear and fiddled with the hem of my short top before continuing. "But above all, I hoped you'd come back for me, even if I'm a self-sabotaging, insecure idiot, because you still think that what we have is special and worth fighting for."

His frown faded, the neutral expression settling back on his face. "Why hope? You said yourself I've been programmed to always come back to you."

I flinched, and then it dawned on me.

He's testing me.

This I could handle. Pushing my shoulders back, I lifted my chin in defiance. "Yes. You were." Kazan narrowed his eyes at me, but I didn't let it faze me. "But since then, you've evolved. I wished you to love no one else but me, you *chose* to make me want no one else but you."

Kazan slightly recoiled, his lips parting in surprise.

"You *chose* to hunt my other Wishes to improve yourself. You *chose* which ones were worthy and which ones were not. But *I* had wished them, which means, in my eyes, they were *all* worthy. You weren't making yourself my greatest Wish but giving yourself the personality of the man you wanted to be and who you believed would also sweep me off my feet. And you succeeded."

I took a few steps towards him under his intense stare, stopping less than two feet away.

"Despite all the times I drifted away from you, instead of fading away like some of my other dreams and wishes, you *chose* to wait for me. You would have waited a human lifespan for me, not because I asked you to, but because you *chose* to. Just like you *chose* to find a way into my world to reach me." I advanced one more step and placed my hands on his waist, relieved he didn't pull away. "You've been here for years, becoming rich and famous, with countless beautiful woman within your grasp. Still, you *chose* me. And now, I hope that, in spite of everything, you came back because you *chose* to fight for us, to fight for me like I'm ready to fight for you."

Kazan's stormy eyes flicked between mine, searching, while I waited for his response with bated breath. His hands cupped my face, and his thumbs caressed my cheeks. My breath hitched.

"I will always fight for you, Jade. I have loved you my entire life, from the awkward teenage girl to the beautiful young woman you've become. In my years on this Mortal Plane, I could have gone for a number of other women, but none of them stir me as only you do. You are my one and only love."

"My Kazan," I whispered as he leaned down to capture my lips.

CHAPTER 10
KAZAN

E yes locked with my woman, I carefully laid her down on my bed, then straightened to discard the bathrobe covering my nudity. Leaning forward, I covered Jade's skin with soft kisses while removing her clothes. No amount of time would diminish my feelings for her or how beautiful she looked to me.

Laying on top of her, I supported my weight on my forearms and brushed my lips against hers. She gazed at me with a look of pure adoration that constricted both my throat and my chest.

"Will you bind me to this realm and let me bind you to mine?" I asked.

She stiffened, a troubled expression fleeting across her face.

"What's wrong?" I asked, my warning bells going off.

"Nothing," she said, averting her eyes.

"Jade, look at me," I ordered in a tone that brooked no argument. She complied, wariness straining her features. "Something just scared you, and it was not my request. I can feel your emotions. What's going on?"

She gave me a pleading look. "Not now, please. Everything is fine. I'll tell you everything but not now. I just got you back. Don't let this spoil our reunion. Please."

I wanted to argue, insist that she tell me the source of her deep fear, but couldn't stand to make her beg. Normally, I would have insisted. However, I didn't feel the presence of any imminent danger, nor did I perceive any such impression from her.

My expression must have shown my surrender because she gave me a grateful smile and drew my face to hers, crushing my lips in a searing kiss.

"Yes, Kazan, I will bind you and let you bind me. You, only you..."

Although her response pleased me, something in her words fueled my feeling of unease. Before I could dwell any further on it, Jade pushed my left shoulder, urging me to roll off of her and onto my back. She immediately climbed on top of me, covering my face, neck, and chest with kisses. It felt wrong to have her pleasing me before I'd satisfied her first, but her intense need to give me pleasure pinned me into place.

And did she ever...

Every time we made love, my human vessel made me reach new highs with the various nuances of sensation; the softness of her skin on mine, the delicious burn of her nails raking down my chest, the heat of her feverish body, the salty taste of her perspiration as she writhed beneath me, the heady scent of her musk and tart taste of her essence, the rapturous sound of her moans, the thundering of her heart... So many subtleties that had eluded me—us—in the Mist Plane.

Even now, the wet heat of her tongue tracing the lines of my abs had my abdominal muscles contracting while blood rushed to my groin. After teasing my navel, Jade's wicked lips continued their path downwards. My body shuddered in anticipation. In her dreams of us, she'd often taken me into her mouth, but in this realm, I had not allowed it, always flipping things around on her any time she'd tried. I hadn't trusted myself not to spill my essence inside her, binding myself to her without consent.

Today, at last, I gave myself over to my mate, a growly moan vibrating in my throat as she rubbed her face against my length with reverence. Her soft fingers caressed my shaft and my balls while her lips freely roamed all over them. The pit of my stomach had transformed into a pool of swirling lava, the heat radiating throughout my groin. When her mouth wrapped around my cock, I nearly died with pleasure. My back arched off the bed with a strangled cry as she bobbed over me, her hand stroking me in counterpoint to the movement of her lips.

The tearing sound of the bed sheet ripping in my fists could barely be heard over my panting moans. I couldn't hold the fire ready to erupt much longer.

"S... stop J-Jade, stop! I... I can't..."

She ignored my garbled plea, encouraged by my pelvis thrusting up with a will of its own into her voracious mouth. It struck me with blinding fury. My body seized painfully, both my seed and part of my ethereal essence pouring out of me and into Jade's mouth in a blistering flow of ecstasy before I collapsed abruptly. My eyes rolled into the back of my head while I trembled. Dazed, it took me a moment to realize that my woman hadn't stopped sucking me even as I wallowed in the throes of passion.

As my cock hardened again under her skillful ministrations, I watched with fascination—and utter joy—the shadow flames of my aura dancing around her head; the perfect crown for my queen. Lifting her head up, she looked at me with hooded eyes, licking her swollen lips before giving me a naughty grin. She climbed on top of me, sitting with our sexes aligned. Lifting my hands to her breasts, she rubbed her core, hot and slick with arousal against my cock, covering it with her essence. While I caressed and kneaded her breasts, she lifted herself slightly before slipping me inside of her.

The feel of her without any barriers nearly undid me again.

My ethereal essence rattled and raged to fill her up and bind me to her, but I held it back. I would see Jade fall apart with pleasure before I allowed myself to topple over again. She rode me with unbridled fury, her hair bouncing in tandem with her breasts as my hands explored her body. My thumb found its way to her clit, rubbing it as she gyrated over me. Jade threw her head back with a throaty moan.

So fucking beautiful.

Despite the inferno building inside of me, I needed more. Drawing her to me, I flipped us around and interlaced my fingers with hers on each side of her face as I thrust into her. So many years I had wished for this moment. Jade was mine, I was hers, and we were one, freely claiming each other.

"I love you," I whispered as sparks of pleasure coursed through my body. "I'm never letting you go."

Picking up the pace, I pounded into her, covering her face with passionate kisses. Jade moaned my name in an endless litany that drove me insane with lust. Her body tensed as she crested, riding the edge, and then falling over with an almost startled cry. I shouted as her inner walls clamped down on me, holding me with a fierce grip that had me groaning in ecstasy with each stroke.

Unable to resist any longer, I roared my release, my seed and ethereal essence erupting inside Jade. I could feel myself coursing through her, surrounded by my mate's vessel, entwined with her every emotion and sensation. My brand tattooed above her breastbone flared and expanded, rooting itself deeper, anchoring me further to my woman and to this world.

Jade writhed beneath me, swept by a whirlwind of pleasure and pain. I took the latter away as I continued to pump in and out of her until I hardened again. Twice more I crested and climaxed in tandem with my mate, before collapsing, spent, and finally, irrevocably bound to Jade.

She snuggled against my side, her face buried in my neck, and her arm possessively wrapped around me.

"I love you, Kazan," she whispered.

My chest tightened and so did my arms around her. She'd wished me. I'd wished us. And now both our wishes had come true.

∿

After that vigorous romp, we got up and took a shower together. Jade insisted on washing my back for me since she'd been unable to access it when she'd bathed me earlier.

As soon as we finished, I lured her to the studio. Monica would be coming later today to pick up the paintings for the exhibit, but I wanted Jade to be the first to see the final six pieces. Discovering that she had honored my wishes and waited for me to show them to her had touched me deeply. These paintings were the culmination of our lives since I first became self-aware. Sharing that with her meant the world to me.

I prided myself on being a strong man, and yet butterflies swarmed my stomach as we approached the paintings hand in hand. Once we stopped before the first one, I turned to peer at my woman. She looked breathtaking, swallowed up in one of my white boho shirts, her lustrous red hair, messed up by my constant fiddling with it, cascading down her back. She bit her bottom lip, the red painted toes of her bare feet curling as she examined the painting.

I held my breath, fighting a surge of panic, until a smile finally stretched her lips.

"This is your dream," she whispered.

"Yes. Ever since the Mist began, I dreamt that one day I would find your shutters opened and that you'd see me, recognize me, and welcome me," I said, looking at the painting of me in my ethereal form pressing my palm against her bedroom window and her pressing hers over mine as we stared longingly at each other.

"Oh!" she said, looking at the second painting. "You made me look so beautiful!"

I grinned broadly, proud of her approval. "I made you the way I see you," I said, caressing her back with a gentle stroke.

It was the first painting we had done, with Jade lying on the Roman bed, the Mistwalker towering over her at the back, the fingertips of his left hand disappearing under the waistband of her thong and the other caressing her cheek with his knuckles. Lips parted, a rapturous expression on her face, she gazed up at the Mistwalker whose yellow eyes glowed with great intensity.

Jade's cheeks reddened as she moved to the third painting, finding herself floating horizontally in the Mist. Mouth open, head thrown back, she shouted in ecstasy as the Mistwalker buried his face between her legs, his shadowy tendrils wrapped around her naked body, like so many vines immobilizing her.

"Our first night after too many years apart," I whispered teasingly in her ear. "Remind me to thank your sister."

She playfully elbowed me, scrunching her face with embarrassment. I chuckled, remembering how much she had resented her treacherous body for yielding so readily. It had only been one month, yet it felt like a lifetime ago.

Jade shuddered upon seeing the fourth one. I tucked her under my arm, and she placed her palm on my stomach. In a loose representation of the attack after our first date, I'd represented the Mistwalker under the yellowish light of a streetlamp in a deserted street otherwise plunged in darkness. Face snarling, razor sharp claws extended in a menacing pose, he faced off with a faceless, brutish enemy with a giant blade while Jade hid behind the shadowy cape of the Mistwalker. Although still shaken by the incident, the absence of fear emanating from her reassured me I hadn't made a mistake including this instant.

"I love this. It's so beautiful," Jade said as we stepped in front of the fifth painting.

It represented our first night together in the Mortal Plane. The Mistwalker lay on his back in Jade's bed, my shadowy aura spreading over the mattress like a dark pool while Jade rode me. Her luminescent skin lit by the moonlight seeping in through the window, and her windblown red hair contrasted sharply with my obsidian silhouette.

"Oh, Kazan," Jade said, her eyes misting as she gazed upon the last painting.

A shadowy boy sat next to a redheaded teenage girl on a toppled over locker. With one hand holding hers, he caressed her hair with the other while she slept on his shoulder. The only light in the dark and dusty room they sat in came from the open trap-door at the top of the staircase behind them. Mist trickled in, surrounding an older version of the young girl. The woman, sitting at the top of the stairs also slept, her head resting on the chest of the Mistwalker lying on the landing and who had wrapped a protective arm over her shoulders.

She turned to face me, lips quivering and eyes blinking rapidly to keep her tears at bay. "I don't deserve you."

Pulling her into my embrace, I brushed my lips against hers, happier than I ever believed possible. "Nobody deserves me more than you. Thanks for making *my dreams* come true."

She gave me a trembling smile, and I leaned forward to kiss her. As I parted my lips to deepen it, the rumbling sound of her stomach growling had my eyes pop open in surprise.

"Oops," she said with a sheepish grin, holding her tummy with both hands.

I threw my head back and burst out laughing.

"Wow! Way to ruin a romantic moment, young lady," I said teasingly before grabbing her hand and leading her out of the studio. "Come on then. Let's go feed you."

With only a few minutes till noon, I decided to make us a

light meal. Later, we could order in for supper since all the meat I had sat in the freezer and would never thaw in time for my mate not to die of hunger.

My hand resting on top of the open fridge door, I perused its contents then looked over my shoulder at Jade, sitting at the breakfast counter.

"I'm afraid the choices are limited, but I can make you an omelet with hash browns, a garnished bagel, or a BLT sandwich," I said.

She stiffened. The haunted look that crossed her features reminded me of the one she'd worn earlier when she asked me not to press her yet.

"What is it, Jade?" I asked.

"Bagel. Garnished bagel will be fine," she said, too quickly.

My eyes narrowed at her, but I held my tongue. Whatever troubled my mate would likely upset me. Not wanting to get into an argument with Jade all but starving, I quickly made her a toasted bagel with chive cream cheese, avocado, tomatoes and bacon, then made myself two BLT sandwiches. The way she frowned at my meal when I laid it on the breakfast counter didn't go unnoticed. After serving us each a tall glass of iced tea, I settled on the stool next to her, and we both dug in.

Until that first bite, I hadn't realized how hungry my vessel was.

How hungry I was.

Now that I was bound to Jade, I would become more and more human with time. Feeding from emotions would no longer suffice as human food would become my main form of sustenance. I needed to start thinking of this body as me instead of a vessel hosting me.

We made small talk during the meal, and Jade drilled me about the upcoming exhibit, asking whether or not I would show myself this time. I never had. While the media considered it my artistic eccentricity, others wondered if I suffered from some kind of deformity which drove me to hide from the public and refuse to have my picture taken or even send one I'd taken myself.

The latter was closer to the truth.

Unless I exercised major control, my shadowy aura tended to show. While human eyes couldn't see it, a camera or mirror might. In this day and age of cellphones and surveillance cameras, traipsing around town had been challenging and quite draining, until Jade. As my anchor, her emotions had fed me enough when walking or shopping together to allow me to contain my aura without depleting my energy too quickly. Now that I was bound to her, only extreme emotions would make it show.

As I planned to make Jade my wife, showing myself with her on my arm at the grand opening would be a nice way to reveal myself and the six centerpieces featuring her. I could already hear Monica's screams once I'd tell her those six were not for sale. The mere fact that they featured the artist's 'fiancé' would significantly increase their value. However, while I didn't mind selling our fantasies, our life wasn't for sale.

Cleaning up after us once we finished our light meal, I asked Jade if she wanted some cookies for dessert. Despite her sweet tooth, she declined, stating she needed to be good while tapping her stomach.

I shook my head and smiled. Jade wasn't fat. I loved her body and especially that she had some meat, contrary to the skinny models who usually posed for me. Leading her by the hand, I took her to the living room and sat her next to me on the couch. That I hadn't pulled Jade onto my lap or spooned with her should make it clear we had something serious to talk about.

She turned her beautiful green eyes towards me, filled with worry.

"I believe you have something to tell me, Jade," I said in a firm but gentle tone.

She licked her lips nervously, and her fingers fiddled with the hem of my shirt covering her. That made me even more concerned.

"Promise me not to lose it, okay?" she asked.

My back stiffened. "That statement makes me want to lose it, Jade. You're freaking me out, right now. What's going on? What happened?" I asked, a sense of impending doom looming over me.

With much reluctance, Jade revealed to me the ordeal she had faced that very morning.

I lost my shit.

She shouldn't have delayed in telling me about this. Even if Morgan didn't have a welcome into my home, the same rules didn't apply to us when in this human form. As a Mist creature, we had no problem entering any place that had an open access, even a private home where we hadn't been invited. As long as the Mist could enter, so could we. But if a place was closed, trying to enter without explicit consent caused us atrocious physical pain. If not for that, Mistbeasts would rampage through the cities and devour the entire population within hours.

I couldn't quite explain why it worked that way, just like I didn't understand why the rifts systematically remained opened between 68 and 72 hours, but they did. No rule books existed for this anomaly or for our powers and limitations. Everything I knew resulted from experimentation or from watching other Mistwalkers usually trying and failing, with the rare successes.

What I did know was that I needed to get to Morgan before the agents. Although grateful to them for rescuing my mate, I should have been by her side, keeping her safe. Instead, I'd been brooding, spitefully ignoring her calls like a petulant child. Through the Veil, I hadn't perceived their urgency; only that she'd attempted to reach me. It had been petty, but I had wanted to let her simmer for a while and see what it felt like to scream and plead for the one you love only to be ignored as I had been so many times throughout the years, sometimes for months or even longer. I'd only meant to teach her to be careful what she wished for, thinking the three days of the Mist would suffice.

Instead, I almost lost her forever.

Morgan had been a thorn in my side from the moment I'd achieved self-awareness. He was vile. The oldest of all her dreams, he'd been too strong for me to defeat at the time. Had I faced off against him, he'd have killed me and absorbed my life force. But I had one infallible weapon to thwart him; Jade's love. I only had to intrude in her nightmares for her attention to shift to me. Every time, she'd run to me, and I'd sweep her into a sunny, happy place, or force her awake if he already had her pinned down. As a creature of darkness, bright lights didn't physically hurt him, but they blinded and disoriented him—a weakness I exploited ruthlessly over the years as I grew strong enough for him to no longer be a threat to me.

Then it had been his turn to hide as feeding from Jade's emotions made me exponentially stronger. But still, he stalked her, his obsession with having my mate at his mercy growing in tandem with his fury at being denied the prize he considered his by rights.

Morgan was no fledgling Mistwalker. Although new to this world, he had gorged on Jade's fear before being driven away. It would sustain him for a few days. As he reveled in other people's terror, I didn't doubt for a moment that he would seek vulnerable, isolated humans to suck dry. No wonder humans had appointed the Men in Black to track the Nightmares that walked the Mortal Plane. If not apprehended quickly, he would leave a trail of desiccated corpses in his wake while seeking a way to abscond with my mate.

In light of his obsession with Jade, he wouldn't bind himself to any other human. If the agents shot him, they would kill his vessel but his ethereal essence would return to the Mist, unless his energy reserves were too depleted to allow him to pierce through the Veil. While not particularly intelligent, too driven by his primal urges, Morgan was no fool either. He'd make sure to keep his levels up at all times. Once returned to the Mist, it would only be a matter of time before he'd hunted enough to come back here after my Jade.

He needed to be removed permanently, in both this world and mine... by me.

Jade apologized profusely for not telling me right away. As much as it had upset me, I could understand how our tense reunion, and the absence of immediate danger, would have made her choose to put it on the backburner. She'd been the victim, and I wouldn't victimize her further by making her feel bad for not wanting to handle it according to my timetable.

A cold shiver ran down my spine every time I thought about what would have befallen her if not for her quick and level-headed thinking. Even weak as he'd been, Morgan would have drained her within an inch of her life, leaving her helpless to fight him off as he indulged in his sick perversions on her.

We spent the next few days following the news closely for any announcement of suspicious deaths or missing persons. To my surprise and both of our relief, there were none. No matter how many times I told Jade that Morgan being loose in the city wasn't her fault, she kept blaming herself for having dreamt him into being in the first place, then to have let him in. A few more hours outside, and he'd have died of exposure.

She recognized the silliness of her reasoning but couldn't help it. No one chose to have nightmares, let alone for them to take form in the Mortal Plane. And not offering assistance to a person in distress would have been criminal.

I didn't believe for one second that Morgan wasn't out there, feeding for the battle he knew would take place between us. What I didn't know was whether the absence of news about a serial killer resulted from the efficient information control work of the Men in Black, or because Morgan was proving far more intelligent and discreet than I would have given him credit for. Either way, Jade would not want me going after him, even less so if she understood that binding me had actually weakened me.

Jade's ability to sleep like the dead proved useful. Every night, as soon as my mate fell asleep, I roamed the streets looking for Morgan. I felt certain he hid during most of the day to hunt at night, except for early mornings and late afternoons in the hope of catching Jade in a vulnerable position on her way to or back from work.

Jade and I had argued quite a bit about her going back to work until the Nightmare was dispatched. She'd given me some nonsense about refusing to be bullied or cowed into hiding. In her mind, holing up at my place equated to giving him power over her, letting him win. While I acknowledged its philosophical merit, when it came to her safety, I didn't give two shits about intangible, psychological victories.

When she wouldn't give in, I made her promise to never leave her workplace unless I was there. An APB had been sent out about Morgan and news bulletins regularly showed a composite sketch based on Jade's description of him, warning the population that he was wanted and dangerous. If he showed his face at her job, he wouldn't be granted access, not that he would be that stupid. Nevertheless, I didn't let her out of my sight anytime she wasn't at work or sleeping in my bed.

A few times, I'd felt his presence when picking her up at day's end or among a crowd when we went out for dinner or on a romantic walk. Morgan was taunting me, baiting me to abandon my mate's side and chase after him.

No fucking chance.

After the first couple of days, he became cocky and removed his glasses when I found him through the throng of pedestrians on our way to a Moroccan restaurant to satisfy Jade's craving for couscous royal. He'd wanted to challenge me and made sure I knew it was him. The idiot had forgotten his face had been plastered all over the city. In no time, he realized he'd drawn suspicious looks from the crowd and made a hasty retreat. It killed me not to chase after him, but I wouldn't leave my mate in a vulnerable position. Thankfully, she hadn't noticed and spent a lovely evening, blissfully unaware of the brewing trouble.

To my chagrin, Friday came rolling in before I could apprehend my nemesis. Monica, marketing guru that she was, made sure to have Jade and me make an Oscar-worthy entrance to the gallery, minus the red carpet... thankfully.

Although I knew myself anchored enough for my aura not to show, I felt on the verge of panic as the flashes of cameras assaulted us when we stepped out of the limousine Monica had appointed for us. Forcing myself to smile as if I did this every day, I placed a possessive hand around Jade's waist and guided her inside.

She received as much, if not even more attention than I. Instead of stirring my jealousy, it made me puff my chest with pride. My Jade looked stunning in her off-the-shoulder sleeve, short, black dress, the low cut exposing my brand over her heart which had gained intricate swirls now that I was bound to her. She used to hide it before. Since we'd sorted things out after the Mist, and now that she'd acknowledged my true nature, Jade seemed to want to flaunt it the way a new bride shows off her engagement ring.

Monica and Jade hitting it off also made me very happy. My agent's beauty could have raised suspicions that our relationship ran deeper than business, but thankfully didn't. Blonde, brown eyed, on the slightly skinny side but with beautiful legs that went on for days, she was a rich daddy's girl who'd been knocked off of her princess pedestal after losing the love of her life. She'd had no experience in the field before meeting me. Impressed by my work, she'd taken me under her wing and, using her charisma and many contacts among the wealthy, Monica had set me onto an early path to success. Helping my career had given her new purpose and distracted her from the pain of losing Donna.

The exhibit proved to be a resounding success. Monica was beside herself when one of the staff informed her that we'd run out of info kits and price lists. It didn't surprise me. The place was packed.

Thankfully, the majority of the patrons showed great restraint while interacting with Jade and me. The most awkward moment occurred when we walked into the back area of the gallery where Jade's six paintings were displayed. A young, hipster couple was staring at The Claiming. Not noticing us approaching behind them, and indifferent to the semi-shocked and semi-amused looks the other patrons gave them, they voiced their impressions of the painting out loud.

"She's fucking gorgeous," the man said. "I wouldn't mind going down on her in that creature's place."

Jade's milky skin turned a bright shade of red which had me biting the inside of my cheeks not to burst out laughing.

"It's not a creature, it's a Mistwalker," his female companion corrected. "And I wouldn't mind being in her place having him devouring me like that."

The man chuckled. "Even with those tentacles trapping her in the Mist?"

"They're not tentacles. That's where I draw the line," the woman said, with a shudder. "But he's made of shadow, so that's all good." She tilted her head to the side while observing the painting. "She really is hot though. I'd probably want to go down on her myself."

A soft gasp escaped Jade's parted lips. This time, I couldn't help laughing. The rumbling sound drew the attention of the raunchy couple whose eyes widened in surprise and a bit of embarrassment at finding us behind them.

"No offense," the man said with a nervous laughter. "These paintings are brilliant Mr. Dale, and your lady is truly stunning."

"Thank you," I said with an indulgent smile before turning to look at a still blushing Jade. "And yes, she is," I added before kissing her temple.

Jade mumbled a shy thank you and pressed herself against me. The couple nodded and moved on to the next painting. A small crowd had gathered in front of Childhood Sweethearts. We joined them, the professional lighting making the colors of the painting pop even more in a solemn kind of way. I gave Jade a side glance and found her absentmindedly tracing the pattern of my brand with her fingertips as she gazed upon the painting, a dreamy smile on her lips.

That pleased me... a lot.

She'd been doing it often this past week. Every time, it reminded me of all my sacrifices and hard work to bring us here, today.

And I'd do it all over again to share these moments with her.

Starting to feel the strain of too much socializing and enter-taining guests, I worked my way through the crowd, dodging where I could and cutting short when I couldn't, leading Jade towards the production office. Hawk-eyed Monica naturally noticed us trying to bail and made a beeline for us. Instead of the scolding and order to 'go and mingle' I expected, she herded us into the office, closed the door and gave me a 'can you believe this shit?' look before pacing the room. How she managed to walk so steadily and effortlessly on those sky-high heels of hers defied logic.

"Sold out. Your fucking collection sold out in two hours. I should have doubled the prices. No, I should have tripled them!"

"Oh my God! That's amazing!" Jade said, pressing her palm to her chest. "Congratulations, babe!"

"Thanks, love," I said, pulling her into my arms.

Naturally, I was proud, even more so because I'd shared this experience with Jade. Still, the success blew my mind. I had thought Monica's prices to be outrageous, but them selling so fast meant she could have indeed doubled the prices and still sold them, though it could have taken a few more days.

"I need one of the centerpieces," Monica said.

"No," I said, my voice taking on a hard edge. "Those are off-limits."

"Kazan…" Monica whined with that 'give me a break' tone.

"I said no, Monica."

She huffed in exasperation. Hands on her hips, she shook her head like she couldn't believe I was doing this to her.

"You realize I received a seven figure offer for Childhood Sweethearts?" she asked.

"Whoa!" Jade whispered.

"I don't care if they offered a billion for it, the answer would still be no, especially with that painting."

"I already broke up two bidding wars tonight," Monica said with a pout. "I'm going to have to deal with at least a couple more before the night is over."

I gave her a mocking smile. "You're already wearing the black leather dress and spiky heels, no one will question you cracking a whip."

Jade chuckled.

"Idiot," Monica said, making a face at me.

I opened my mouth to tease her some more but the words died on my tongue as the sizzling wave of Mistwalker energy made my small hairs stand on end.

Morgan.

"I need to step out for a few minutes," I said, trying to keep my expression neutral.

"What?" Jade asked, giving me a stunned look. "Where are you going?"

"I just need to take care of something. I'll return soon," I said, casting Monica a meaningful glance. She blanched and nodded. "Don't leave the gallery, okay?" I said to Jade, making it clear I meant business.

"Of course not," she said. "But—"

"I'll be back soon," I said, interrupting her as his presence grew stronger. I didn't want her feeling him. "I love you, Jade."

Kissing her lips one last time, I rushed out of the room.

I exited the building through the back, using my temporary, all-access pass which prevented the alarm from going off. As an organizer of the exhibit, I needed access to the docking and loading area to receive or ship pieces for the show. The delivery courtyard connected three other buildings; an art school, the museum, an art workshop that specialized in repairing and restoring paintings, and the gallery, forming a large arena. Being well after hours, the delivery courtyard was plunged in darkness except for dim lights by the docking doors and back entrance— an ideal setting for Morgan.

The unusual shapes created by the back of the buildings provided much cover and shadow to lurk in, thanks to the moonless night. While I couldn't see him, the weight of his stare and the slimy energy of his presence settled over me like so many creepy crawlers.

"Ever the coward, hiding in the shadows instead of facing me," I said tauntingly, knowing he could see me.

The tingling sensation increased as his temper flared, drawing me towards his location.

"Come out, come out and play," I teased, leisurely strolling towards him. "But then, you only attack those you think weaker than you. It must have stung that inflated ego of yours to get spanked by the girl you thought would be easy prey."

"She didn't defeat me!" he shouted from the shadows, the sound emanating from a corner of the workshop.

Gotcha!

"Oh but she did. Outsmarted and outfought you," I said,

pouring as much contempt as I could into my voice. "My Jade had you on your knees, crying like a baby, pissing blood all over the place. What a pathetic big bad wolf you make."

"She's MY Jade, you usurper. She didn't make me cry. This pathetic vessel turned on me," he spat, stepping out of the shadows.

As my eyes adjusted to the darkness, aided by the faint glow of the docking lights, I recognized the human appearance he'd often used when hunting Jade as a slasher. Handsome, with a body similar in size and shape to mine, he only fit Jade's more superficial preferences in men. It pissed me off to realize he'd taken my black denim jeans which were Jade's favorite. I felt violated that he should wear them and would make certain to replace them without her knowing. His hoodie was new. Considering the cut she'd inflicted on him, my shirt he'd borrowed must have been rendered unusable from blood stains. I didn't want to think about the poor victim he'd stolen the hoodie from.

I nonchalantly slipped my hands into my pockets as I slowly advanced towards him. I fingered the extra bright pocket flashlight I'd been carrying religiously during my nightly hunts, ready to whip it out at a moment's notice. With over 400 lumens, it was bright enough to blind an opponent even in broad daylight. With him, I had no qualms playing dirty, especially since his ethereal strength would exceed mine now that I was bound. But I had the terrain advantage, having tamed my human vessel, mastered its weaknesses, and learned the best ways to leverage my ethereal power when battling as an earthbound man.

"Jade was never yours, you vermin," I said, deliberately riling him. Anger made people act without thought—especially him. "Her only wish concerning you was to never see you again."

"Because of you!" he shouted, his shadowy aura spreading around him.

Good. Waste your energy.

"You greedy little shit. I would have shared her with you. But no, you needed to hog her all to yourself, stealing her from me and interfering in our time together!"

"You would have shared what?" I asked with contempt. "The broken, scarred husk of Jade? I couldn't have taken her if she had wanted you. She *wished* me and, above all, she wished me to take her away from the Nightmare. You lost her by your own actions, by your lust for her pain and terror."

"There is pleasure in pain," Morgan argued.

The front of his pants strained as thoughts of Jade's pain—no doubt—excited him. It made me sick to my stomach.

"She hates pain!" I spat, fisting the flashlight in my pocket.

"She'll learn to love it. I'll make sure of it," Morgan said with an evil grin. "But first, you die, little brother."

"I'm no brother of yours," I said, whipping out the flashlight as he lunged at me.

He shouted, closing his eyelids and averting his face as the bright light stabbed his eyes, allowing me to easily dodge his blow. Pressing my advantage, I wrapped an ethereal glove around my fist, which I threw at him. Although still blinded and blinking, Morgan raised his palm in the trajectory of my fist, stopping it before howling in pain. I felt the bones crushing in his hand with the impact.

Despite the pain, Morgan reacted like a wounded beast by lashing out with a fist. I tried to get out of its path, but it solidly connected with my left side. The blow took my breath away as my opponent had put his ethereal strength behind it. I staggered a few steps back, holding my side. Had I not shielded my human form with my ethereal aura, Morgan would have not only broken my ribs, chances were he'd have punched right through skin and bones, smashing my internal organs in the process. Instead, the Nightmare had smashed the bones of his own hand, not having shielded it with his aura. His knees buckled, and his eyes rolled back in his head from the pain as he struggled to remain conscious.

I seized the opportunity to regain my breath. Morgan's blow would leave a bad bruise on my side that I'd have a hard time explaining to Jade. Being bound to her, using my ethereal aura as armor or to battle, depleted me quickly. A few more such blows would leave me completely vulnerable. But as I had hoped, being newborn to this world, Morgan hadn't learned how to shield his vessel. The humans he would have hunted over the past five days would have been paralyzed with fear upon seeing his aura, making them easy victims to his superior strength.

"So, *brother*," I said with contempt, "are you finding much pleasure in this pain?"

Despite my urge to finish him and in spite of his broken hands, Morgan's ethereal form remained too strong. Trusting in his apparent vulnerability would be my downfall. I needed him to shed even more of his reserves before I went in for the kill. Had I not been bound, he'd already be dead.

"I'm going to kill you, Kazan Dale," Morgan hissed with such hatred my skin crawled.

The sight of his human eyes glowing freaked me out for a second before realizing his Mistwalker form had surged forth. This was what I'd hoped for. His energy would drain very quickly, but he would be deadlier and faster than before.

He charged me. I blinded him again, making Morgan falter and avert his eyes while I moved out of range. After repeating this a couple of times, he finally caught on to my game. Shadowy tendrils protruded from his aura, similar to the ones I'd restrained Jade with on our first night in the Mist. When he next lunged for me, he whipped them in my direction. While I avoided most of them as I blinded him, a couple tendrils found their mark with the burning sting of a lash.

Grinding my teeth through the pain, I continued to kite him around as he depleted his reserves, taking my licks until I felt him weakened enough to go on the offensive. The next time he lashed at me, I held onto one of his tendrils and sucked the life force out of him. In his panic, he didn't think to drain me in return but fought to free himself, trying to pull away. He whipped at me, but I let go and stepped back to avoid the blows. I'd taken too many already but his life force, slimy though it was, gave me a boost to replenish my shielding aura.

I advanced on him, drawing on his life force. When he whipped his tendrils at me to keep me at bay, I caught as many as I could and jerked him towards me. This time, he sucked at my life force. With my free hand, I punched his human body beneath his Mistwalker aura, using the maximum ethereal strength possible without hurting myself. Morgan clawed at me with his ethereal hands, forcing me to let go.

Every time Morgan managed to free himself of my hold, I verbally taunted him before resuming the chase, pummeling and draining him.

"You should have fought me in the Mist when you had the chance rather than cowering away. This is my world now. You don't attack a Hunter in his own territory," I said, before charging him.

For the first time, I read true fear in his glowing, yellow eyes. Morgan had never imagined defeat to be possible, having always crushed his prey in the past. He was staring into true death's eyes, knowing there would be no mercy from me.

The force of the impact as my body collided with his knocked him off his feet. His already injured human vessel writhed from the shock. Morgan choked my neck with his ethereal hands while his tendrils wrapped around me to crush me while sucking my life force. But they were too weak to break through my shielding aura. Fisting his human form's hair, I smashed the back of his head repeatedly on the asphalt. Dazed, his hold weakened until it dropped.

"You shouldn't have come after my woman," I hissed in his face. "Now you die."

"Nooo!" Morgan pleaded in a pained whisper.

Heedless of his final word, I sucked the life force from him, watching his ethereal aura turn to ashes while his human vessel withered to a shriveled husk.

No one threatened my woman.

CHAPTER 11
JADE

I frowned at the door through which Kazan had all but fled the office.

"Well, that was odd," I mumbled.

Monica chuckled and walked towards the mini fridge.

"You're dating an odd man. Him acting weird is normal."

I scrunched up my face. "Yeah, I guess."

Pulling up one of the chairs, I all but collapsed into it and rubbed my ankles. It had been a while since I'd worn fuck-me shoes. Although they gave me killer legs, they wrecked my back and feet. Casting a furtive glance at Monica as she grabbed some mineral water from the mini-fridge, I couldn't help but admire her ease on her even higher heels. She waved a bottle at me with a questioning look on her pretty face.

"Yes, please," I said with gratitude, suddenly realizing how parched my throat felt.

I hadn't known what to expect when Kazan had first told me about his agent. Monica didn't have a classic beauty, her features were lacking a bit of symmetry for that, but her inner strength and confidence gave her an irresistible allure. At first glance, I feared she'd be the tough, bitchy chick, used to having things her own way. She was, but thankfully without the bitchy part. Platinum blonde—though her darker eyebrows suggested her to be a brunette instead—she couldn't be taller than 5'1, which probably explained those stilts she called high heels. Although on the skinny side with delicate bird bones, Monica didn't inspire the instinct to protect but to watch out, because she'd kick your ass if you crossed her.

I liked her.

Monica and Kazan's visibly friendly—but unmistakably platonic—relationship did wonders to alleviate my resurfacing insecurities. Having met some of the other models in the exhibition hall had made me feel incredibly self-conscious. They were as gorgeous in person as in their paintings. Despite Kazan swearing up and down that he hadn't enhanced me, just painted me the way he saw me, I feared the patrons would call me out for a fraud when they saw the real me compared to the paintings. To my relief, they'd either been too polite, or they hadn't given a shit. The latter was probably the case.

"Thank you," I said to Monica as she handed the bottle over.

I opened it and guzzled down half of it. Monica laughed again while sitting on top of the desk at my right. I turned slightly on my chair to face her, intrigued by the assessing look she was giving me.

"He's crazy about you, you know?" Monica asked, although it came out as more of a statement. "I mean, head-over-heels in love with you."

My face heated, and my chest warmed. "I don't quite get why," I said shyly, "but I'm grateful because I'm bonkers for him, too. No man has ever treated me so wonderfully or understood me as completely as he does. He's perfect."

She smiled, but I didn't miss the flicker of sadness that crossed her brown eyes. "Of course, he is," she said wistfully. "All Wishes are."

I stiffened, and my gaze flicked up to hers. She held it

without flinching, her lips stretching into a strange smile I didn't know how to interpret. Pulling down the zip of her sleeveless, form-fitting, black leather top with one hand, she spread the collar open with the other, revealing a brand over her heart, similar to mine in style but depicting a different symbol. My jaw dropped, followed by a sharp intake of breath.

Mind racing, I cycled through my memories of the guests for any dreamy looking man who would have shadowed Monica with the same possessiveness Kazan did me but came up empty.

"Who—?"

"She's dead," Monica interrupted before I could complete my sentence.

I covered my mouth with my hand, my chest constricting, and my heart filling with compassion for her. I couldn't even begin to imagine losing Kazan.

Wait. What does she mean by dead?

"Dead, as in…?" I asked, kicking myself for the insensitive way my mouth just blurted it out.

"As in permanently," she said, devoid of emotion.

"I'm sorry. I didn't…"

"Don't worry," Monica said with a dismissive wave of her small hand, her long, manicured nails painted with black nail polish. "It happened over seven years ago thanks to a bunch of stupid frat boys DUI. We weren't even driving, just strolling on the sidewalk. The kid lost control, then bumped into another car before crashing into a shop. It was the other car spinning from the impact that hit Donna. She died in my arms."

Monica's voice choked on those last words.

"I'm so very sorry," I said, not knowing what to do. I wanted to go give her a hug but somehow suspected she wouldn't welcome it.

"I know what you're thinking," Monica said with a tired voice. "Why didn't I wish her back?"

I bit my lip and nodded. The thought had indeed crossed my mind.

"I did, but it doesn't work that way. Once a Mistwalker meets true death, it's over. If you want it hard enough, another Wish will spark that may or may not achieve self-awareness. But when it does, the chances that it will develop the exact same person-ality as the previous one are slim to none."

Monica ran her fingers through her shoulder-length, curly, blond hair, her expression distant as she reminisced.

"In many ways, Donna's death had been a mercy for her, and an eye opener that came too late for me." Monica smiled sadly at my confused expression. "I was a self-centered, spoiled, rich daddy's girl. Being a lesbian didn't fit into Dad's perfect plans for me, but as long as I remained discreet with my relationships, he didn't give me a hard time. A few months after the rifts first opened, I'd spent the Mist with a bunch of friends at Simon's house. He's an investment banker, the son of my dad's partner. He'd just replaced his windows with bulletproof glass so that we could leave the shutters up and safely admire the freak show outside."

Monica snorted in self-derision then took a swig from her bottle of water. From the look on her face, she could have used something far stronger.

"That's when I met Donna for the first time. I had no idea she was a female when the dark wraith made a beeline for me. It freaked us all out at first but then everyone teased me about a demon having the hots for me. She was creepy, and yet she fasci-nated me. See, unlike you and Kazan, I have zero interest in fantasy and fairy tales. I'm the hardcore evolutionist and scien-tific type. Having a mythical creature in my life didn't compute."

The petite woman took another long sip of water, screwed the lid on, and fiddled with the bottle pensively.

"For the three days at Simon's, the Mistwalker just followed me around, wherever there was a window that allowed her to see me. By the next Mist, I'd installed bulletproof windows in my own flat, unable to forget about the strange creature. And sure enough, there she was. It took me two more Mists to finally gather the courage to let her in."

Monica's index finger absentmindedly traced the pattern of her brand the same way I often did. My heart ached again for her.

"I hated when she took me into the Mist. It messed with my head. As much as I loved being with her, that place was too much for me. I was such a selfish princess. Everything had to be about me. I bound her to me and then, not content with having forced her to forfeit the Mist in favor of a uniquely human life, I also made her change her real name Adoan to Donna, to make it more 'normal' sounding. I treated her like a simple friend in public, forbidding her any public displays of affection. To make me happy, she took it all. The more human she became, the more miserable she was because of my treatment of her. I knew it but turned a blind eye, too happy in my own little bubble."

Monica fiddled some more with the bottle, lost in thought before plopping it next to her on top of the desk. Locking eyes with me, she gripped the edge of the desk with both hands.

"If death hadn't claimed Donna, she would have left me regardless because I treated her like shit. It took that tragedy for me to understand she was my partner, not my pet or my property. For months after her passing, I scoured the streets and homeless refuges looking for her until I had to accept that she was gone. One day, at the county fair, I felt the Mistwalker tingle again. It was different, but I wanted to believe she'd come back to me. Instead, I found a giant man in clothes too small for him, sketching people for a pittance."

"Kazan," I whispered.

She smiled. "Yep, your Kazan. I initially took him under my wing as a way to make amends for my Donna. But in truth, he helped me get my life together far more than I helped him. He has an amazing talent and would have succeeded either way, if only by sheer determination to make something of himself that was worthy of you."

My throat tightened as my heart filled with love for my wonderful man.

"I've never seen Kazan happier than he's been since he has finally reached you. Thank you for being smarter than me and realizing the gem you have. He's the best of men."

I nodded, my eyes misting.

A soft knock at the door startled us both. I blinked the tears away before they could fully form. Monica pushed her shoulders back and lifted her chin, becoming once again the no-nonsense tough girl that I'd met earlier.

"Come in!" she called out.

The door opened, and one of the hostesses peeked her head in. "Sorry to disturb you, Ms. Sheffield, but you are being requested at the exhibit."

"I'll be there in a minute," Monica answered.

As soon as the door closed, she jumped to her feet and gave me a serious look.

"By the fancy detailing on your brand, I can tell that you've bound Kazan. You *must* let him return to the Mist every month for the three days it lasts to replenish his ethereal essence. The longer he remains in our world, the more human he will become. If he dies, it will be permanent."

I nodded, my stomach knotting with anxiety. "I promise. In fact, I already agreed to let Kazan bind me to him in his world at the next Mist."

The smile she gave me was a strange mix of sisterly gratitude, sadness, and envy. With a final nod, she walked out, leaving me alone in the office. I stared at the door long after it had closed behind her.

~

More than half an hour had gone by before Kazan finally returned. I'd been on the verge of sending a search party after him. When he walked in with his shirt and pants almost in tatters by what looked like whiplashes, I nearly lost it.

"Oh my God, Kazan! What happened to you?" I asked, running up to him.

"I'm fine. Everything is fine now," Kazan said with a soothing voice.

"What the fuck do you mean, you're fine? Your clothes are torn to shreds. Did you get attacked? Are these bruises?" I asked, frantically pawing at him to lift the rags of his shirt only to find a network of darkening bruises and red welts all over him. "Oh God!" I whispered in horror. "What the hell did this to you?"

Then a cold shiver ran down my spine as the tingle of an ethereal presence wrapped around me. I recognized it as Kazan's but yet, not. It held a slimy, evil undertone I'd only felt once before that made my skin crawl.

Tearing my hands away from him as if they'd been burnt, I took a few steps back, fear rising from deep within.

"Who are you?" I whispered, casting furtive glances around the room while keeping him in my line of sight, looking for something to use as a weapon.

Kazan froze, taken aback by my question. In light of his genuine confusion, I wondered if my paranoia had me overreacting. But after Morgan, I would never ignore my instincts again.

"You don't feel like my Kazan," I said, taking another step back. "There's something off about you."

From the expression on his face, understanding dawned on him.

"You're right, there is something off about me," he said in a reasonable tone. "Please do not fear me, my Jade. It is me, your Kazan."

That he didn't try to approach me further alleviated some of my fears, and the feel of Kazan gradually overpowered the lurking sliminess beneath his energy.

"Our first physical meeting was in a grocery store," Kazan said. "On our first date, I realized Sangria and barbecue ribs are far too sweet in this world. You're more ticklish behind your left knee than your right." Pointing at my feet, he continued, "You don't like wearing heels this high but insisted on wearing them tonight because you wanted to look your best to make me proud. Except, I'm always proud of you, Jade."

Relief flooded me that it was indeed my man, but... then he confessed to having battled Morgan.

I lost it.

Kazan literally had to pin me against the wall to calm me down when I upended my purse in a total state of panic, looking for Agent Thomson's card. How the fuck had I not sensed he'd been in danger or been overwhelmed by the tingle of Morgan's presence? I remembered how strong Kazan's aura had been when he'd battled those thugs on our first date. With both Kazan and Morgan exuding this much energy, I should have felt it.

Finding out he'd killed Morgan further rattled my confused emotions. I didn't care that he'd killed to eradicate that menace but feared the potential legal repercussions. If we confessed to the Fourth Division, presented it as the self-defense it had been, surely they'd press no charges and close the case. After all, Kazan had done their job for them. Right?

Having hidden the corpse in the shadows of the buildings, where unaware humans were unlikely to find him in, Kazan promised to inform Agent Thomson once he had me safely back home. Too numb from shock, I didn't argue. As he couldn't be seen in public with the current state of his clothes, Monica came to the rescue by calling the chauffeur to pick us up at a side exit. Proving as efficient as Kazan had praised her to be, she miraculously found him a long jacket that covered the worst of his ruined clothes.

Although he put up a good front, Kazan's wounds clearly pained him. As soon as we got home, I drew him a warm bath while he contacted the Fourth Division. When I came back out of the bathroom to get him, I found him staring at his phone with a frown.

"What's wrong?" I asked. "You can't reach Agent Thomson?"

"No," Kazan said with a troubled look on his face. "I didn't want to be drawn into a lengthy discussion so I just texted him the location of Morgan's remains and said I'd call him in the morning. He texted back that they were already done."

"What? How?" I asked, stunned.

"He only said that our power surges gave us away."

"They can track that?" I asked.

"Yes," Kazan said with a slow nod. "The same with our birth into human form. I just didn't realize they could do so with such accuracy."

"Well, at least, that's one Nightmare taken care of for good," I said, pun intended, in a lame effort to lighten the mood. "But now, let's take care of you."

Kazan smiled and walked up to me. Taking the hand I'd extended towards him, he let me lead him into the bathroom. My stomach knotted and my eyes pricked upon seeing the extent of the damage he'd sustained as I helped him out of his clothes.

"It's okay, my Jade. It will heal."

"You could have died!" I said accusingly. "I could have lost you without even having a chance to say goodbye."

Thoughts of Monica and Donna flashed through my mind, and I shuddered.

"But I didn't," Kazan said in an appeasing tone, holding my shoulders with both hands. "The Men in Black failed to capture him for five days, making you a prisoner. Even if they had caught him, they'd only have sent him back to the Mist Plane, and we would have spent the following months worrying about when he'd reappear. You and I both know Morgan would never have stopped chasing you. Only I could take him out."

"But... but you're bound now. You could have permanently died! You should have told me!"

Kazan cupped my face between his hands, a sliver of guilt flickering through his stormy eyes.

"Which is why I needed to do it now," he said gently. "The last Mist was only five days ago. Having spent the whole three days there, I had plenty of time to replenish my reserves. Waiting a full month for the next Mist would have put us both at too great a risk because I would have been too weak by then to protect either of us. I also didn't want to lose my advantage." He smiled at my questioning look. "I know how to function in this world and how this body works," he added waving at himself. "He was still learning, which also gave you the edge when he attacked you on Monday."

Shoulders sagging, I sighed and nodded. My head understood his logic, but it would take a while for my emotions to fully recover from this.

"Let's get you into that bath before the water grows cold," I said, helping him in.

"Join me," he said, after settling himself in the tub.

"This is for you to relax and soothe your aches and pains," I argued weakly.

"I'll relax better with my woman in my arms," he said with a smile.

I caved and joined him, grateful for the large Jacuzzi-style bath. We soaked in the warm water more than we actually bathed. When it began to cool, we got out and made a beeline for the bed. I'd never seen Kazan this worn out. Although he wouldn't go into details about the fight, it had visibly taken a lot out of both his ethereal and human forms. At least, he reassured me that he'd only absorbed Morgan's life force, not his personality or traits like he had my *lesser* Wishes.

To my great distress, Kazan had nothing worth calling a medical kit, possessing only a bottle of peroxide, a bag of cotton balls, and a box of bandages. Thankfully, I always carried some painkillers in my purse and gave him a couple with some water before tucking him in. Despite the extensive contusions all over his body, he insisted on holding me in his arms while we slept.

The next morning, Kazan's bruises had further darkened. This time, he didn't pretend not to be in pain. For a moment, I feared he'd sustained some internal damage or fractures that might need medical attention. He insisted it wasn't the case and that time would make it all better. I gave him more painkillers and brought my man a light breakfast in bed which I ended up feeding to him after he winced while trying to raise the fork to his lips. I loved taking care of Kazan. He enjoyed it, too, yet felt self-conscious to appear so weak before me.

Silly man.

"I'm going to run down to the pharmacy to get you some pain, bruise and swelling cream, and some stronger painkillers," I said, leaning over to kiss his lips as he lay back down at the end of his meal.

Worry flashed through his eyes.

"Morgan is dead, remember? I'm safe now, thanks to you."

Kazan sighed then nodded.

"You rest your handsome head while I'm out. I'll drop by the grocery store on my way back and grab some buttery popcorn for moi and a huge bag of kettle-cooked salt and vinegar chips for you."

He beamed at me through heavy eyelids.

"Sleep, my love," I said, kissing his forehead. "I'll be back soon."

Kazan was out like a light before I even closed the bedroom door behind me. Grabbing the keys to his car, I exited the apartment, the door automatically locking behind me. On my way down to the underground parking, I called Monica to give her an update and inform her that Kazan wouldn't be able to come for the business wrap up of the exhibit planned for later that day. She understood, of course, and said it actually suited her because it would give her more time to study and organize the awesome opportunities that had been presented to her by parties interested in working with Kazan.

Walking up to the car, I hung up, dropped my phone in my purse, and used the remote to unlock the door. As I reached for the handle, movement at the edge of my vision followed by the sound of a car door closing made me look up. My heart skipped a beat as I recognized Agent Wilkins and another agent I didn't know walking towards me from the familiar black car I had seen following Kazan at the shopping mall. One hand gripping the strap of my purse while the other fisted my keys which dug into my palm, I waited, heart pounding as they closed the distance between us.

"Ms. Eastwood," Agent Wilkins said with a cold and commanding voice, "we need you to come with us back to head-quarters."

My stomach dropped, a sense of dread building within. "Why?" I asked. "What do you want with me?"

"Please do not make this difficult or your situation worse by resisting arrest," Wilkins said in a clipped tone.

"Arrest?" I exclaimed, winded. "Arrest for what?"

"We need to question you about your connection with the death of the serial killer Morgan Doe and the multiple victims he left behind."

"All right. All right. I'll come with you, but I need to warn—"

"What you need to do is to follow us before I drag you in," Wilkins said, taking a menacing step towards me.

"You haven't read me my rights, and I'm entitled to a lawyer!" I exclaimed taking a step back.

"Do I look like your fucking local sheriff? We're dealing

with matters of national security which *you* have jeopardized with your sick fantasies. You have no fucking rights except the ones we give you."

Before I could react, he ripped my purse out of my grasp and handed it to his partner who watched us impassively. My eyes widened as I recognized him as one of the guests at the exhibit last night. There would be no help coming from him. Grabbing my forearm in a bruising hold, Wilkins shoved me towards his car.

"Now start walking if you don't want me to drag you," Wilkins snapped.

Stumbling forward, I managed to keep my balance and turned around to argue. At the sight of his hand resting on his gun belt and his thumb flicking open the safety strap, the words I'd been meaning to speak died on my tongue. Swallowing hard, I complied and walked up to their car, my mind racing.

Wilkins stuffed me into the back of the car and raised the protective glass between us the minute I asked about Agent Thomson. The older agent had been respectful and professional, seemingly the one to keep Wilkins in check. I'd feel safer with him present. The nameless agent who now held my purse didn't get in the car right away. I couldn't see him from where I sat. About four minutes later, he returned from whatever errand he'd run. The horrible thought that he might have rigged Kazan's car with explosives popped into my head but then I dismissed it. The Men in Black were all about discretion and keeping the public in a state of blissful ignorance. An explosion would draw too much attention on top of the potential collateral damages and casualties if one of the neighbors happened to be nearby when it detonated.

With the two men still ignoring me, we drove off. My anxiety levels rose as we left City Center from where most governmental agencies operated and headed towards the industrial sector of town. Where my vivid imagination served me well as a game artist, right now, I could have done without all the nightmarish scenarios flashing through my mind.

My heart pounded as we drove into the underground parking garage of a large, square building, with dark walls and tinted windows. No logo or sign outside indicated its nature. If not for the Men in Black driving me into it now, I would have assumed it to be an extension of the well-known pharmaceutical research facility it was appended to. That further raised my anxiety level, imagining what kind of more secretive experiments could be happening there with such neighbors.

As soon as we parked, Wilkins took me in to have my mugshot, fingerprints, and even a picture of my brand taken before having his buddy take me into one of the interrogation rooms. Once more, they ignored my requests for a phone call or for a lawyer's assistance. Along the way, I hadn't failed to notice that only a handful of people were on the premises—none of whom were Agent Thomson. Not really surprising considering it was still early morning on a Saturday.

Wilkins' buddy, who couldn't be bothered to give me his name, made me take a seat inside the typical interrogation room; off-white walls, light-grey tiled floors, completely empty aside from the single table with a couple of chairs, and the traditional one-way mirror. Thankfully, he didn't shackle me, content to tell me to keep my ass seated before walking out.

At least ten minutes went by while I squirmed on the highly uncomfortable metal chair and imagined increasingly bad scenarios which fed the stress twisting me inside out. It was still too early for Kazan to start worrying about my absence. Worse still, considering his exhaustion level, he would probably sleep for many more hours.

The door opened abruptly to reveal Wilkins, startling me. He strutted in with a smug look on his face, a bottle of water held in his hand. Instead of taking a seat on the chair on the opposite side of the table, he stood next to it and towered over me. I realized in that instant that he took pleasure in intimidating people and making them feel inferior; a typical bully. I wouldn't indulge his sick games. Lifting my head defiantly, I held his gaze, unflinching. He opened his bottle and took a large swig before staring me again in the eyes.

"What do you want from me? Where's Agent Thomson?" I asked.

"You don't ask the questions here, Ms. Eastwood. I do," Wilkins said, injecting as much contempt as he could into my name.

"Then ask them and stop with the stupid mind games," I spat.

He slammed his fist on the metal table, making me flinch, but I still refused to let myself be intimidated.

"You better check that attitude after the shit-storm you caused, you little freak!" the agent hissed.

My breath hitched as I stared at him, disbelieving. "What shit-storm? I haven't done anything!"

"Really?" he asked, circling around the table to stand at an uncomfortably close distance from my chair. "What about the thirteen people who have died because of that monster you summoned?"

Oh God! Thirteen?

My heart broke at the thought of so many innocents perishing, especially knowing Morgan wouldn't have given them a swift death; not the way he reveled in other people's pain. I hugged myself and swallowed painfully.

"The news didn't mention…"

"Because we cleaned up after your fucking Nightmare and spun somewhat believable tales to those poor families. How many more sick fantasies have you unleashed on this world?"

"I didn't unleash anything! Nobody has control over their Nightmares, let alone on whether or not they decide to crossover. How do you know your own worst fears aren't roaming the streets?"

Leaning forward, he placed his hands on each arm of my chair and shouted, "I know because I'm the one hunting these beasts to keep humans safe."

I turned my face away from him, sickened by his closeness and the spittle flying from his infuriated shout. He seemed possessed.

"The only things I've found are the abominations deviant freaks like you dream up," he said before pushing himself back up, rocking my chair.

Heart pounding, I watched him from the corner of my eye as he circled around me, the weight of his hatred crushing me. What the fuck had I ever done to that man to be treated like this?

"But that's not enough for you fanatics, is it?" Wilkins said, eyeing me with disgust. "First you bring that demon over to satisfy your sick sexual fantasies. We agreed to look the other way. Then you bring that serial killer. And now you spread abhorrent propaganda to lure good, innocent girls into your life of debauchery and unnatural couplings. YOU and demented zealots like you are responsible for Mist Pacts."

Throughout his tirade, I stared at him in an utter state of shock.

He's insane.

He called me the fanatic, but his eyes held the mad glimmer of a rabid bigot.

"Propaganda? What are you talking about?"

"We saw your abhorrent paintings at that farce you called an exhibit, promoting perverse couplings between women and beasts. But you had to cross the line and romanticize human females getting defiled by Mist demons."

Wilkins thankfully moved away from me and circled around the table, his fingertips drumming on its surface then gliding as he advanced before drumming again. There was something mentally disturbed about his behavior.

"It… it's just art!" I argued. Although it seemed insane to me that anyone could think Kazan and I were promoting Mist Pacts in any way, I could see how someone like him and conspiracy theorists might. "There are tons of artists painting Mistwalkers in a non-threatening and even good light."

"Nobodies!" Wilkins yelled. "Not influencers like your demon! Agent Tate secretly recorded multiple conversations between patrons expressing envy towards the models in the paintings, some going as far as stating that they just might let one Mistwalker in for a try."

I huffed and threw my hands up in exasperation. "That just silly small-talk. Stand outside a movie theater after a fantasy or sci-fi movie just played and see how many women will fantasize about the characters, both heroes and villains. That doesn't mean they wouldn't run for the hills if an actual vampire or alien came knocking on their door!"

"We'll see if you'll still call it small-talk when you get indicted for incitement to suicide after a bunch of these women go missing at the end of the next Mist. Back in the day, they knew how to handle whores who consorted with demons."

"You are insane! You want to burn me at the stake because—"

The door bursting open made me squeal in surprise. Then hope blossomed in my heart.

"What the fuck is going on here?" Agent Thomson demanded. From his casual civilian clothes, I suspected he hadn't expected to come in to work. "Why is she here?"

Although Wilkins lifted his chin defiantly, I didn't miss the flicker of unease in his crazy eyes.

"Bait," he said, standing his ground.

"Bait for what?" Agent Thomson asked, completely confused.

"For that abomination she's fucking. He broke the agreement. He forfeited the right to stay in this world!"

Agent Thomson recoiled. "What?"

"He swore not to drain or kill anyone in our world!"

I gasped, unable to believe what I was hearing. "Are you fucking kidding me?" I asked. "He did *your* job for you, better than you ever could have by ensuring Morgan can never come back."

"He broke the agreement!"

"Fuck your agreement! You should kiss his feet and thank him for making sure the death count won't go over thirteen."

"Shut your fucking mouth, you cunt. I..."

Wilkins threat died in a gurgle, his face turning red as Agent Thomson fisted his collar, tightly enough to strangle him.

"That's enough!" Thomson shouted, his face inches from his partner's. "You and I need to talk. Get your ass to my office," he added, shoving Wilkins towards the door.

The younger man adjusted his white shirt and black suit, before loosening his black tie. After casting a murderous glance in my direction, he walked out without a word. Agent Thomson ran a nervous hand through his greying hair, mumbling under his breath something I didn't understand.

"I'm sorry for all this, Ms. Eastwood," he said, worry and sympathy oddly mingling in his baby blue eyes. "I will return shortly to sort this all out."

"Okay. Thank you," I said. "Can I make a phone call?"

"In a minute. Let me handle this idiot and then we can fix this whole mess," he said, then walked out, closing the door behind him without giving me a chance to answer.

It would be closer to twenty minutes before Agent Thomson returned with grim news. Apparently, he'd tried to reach Kazan but got no response. After the agent had returned my phone to me, I found a dozen missed calls from Kazan, then the single text message stating: "I'm coming for you."

CHAPTER 12
KAZAN

I snapped awake with an uneasy feeling. In all my time in the Mortal Plane, I'd never had an actual nightmare. My latest dream had been strange but not terrifying. I hated not remembering it in this realm, only retaining a lingering feeling of what had transpired. At least, sleeping as a human gave me a small window into the Mist which, in turn, permitted me to syphon some sliver of ethereal energy back. It also used to do wonders in healing my human vessel, but binding myself to Jade had a cost which I felt now. Although I didn't regret it, I'd become more human, and my ethereal magic didn't work as well, healing me far less than it used to.

My entire body still ached. Muscles I hadn't even known existed screamed their displeasure. As I rolled to my side to find a more comfortable position, the sense of unease I now realized had been nagging me even in my sleep poked and prodded at me again. Looking at the clock, I quickly assessed that Jade had gone out about forty minutes ago.

"Jade," I called out, wondering if she had already returned.

When complete silence met my shout, I focused on that disturbing feeling that something was off. Back in the Mist, it usually happened when Jade was hurt, in trouble, or pursued by a Nightmare. With Morgan having met his permanent death, I couldn't imagine what could provoke this sense of doom in the Mortal Plane.

Picking up my phone, I checked for any messages from Jade. Finding none, I called her only to land in her voicemail. Knowing how she often tossed her phone into her purse, then had to rummage to fish it out, I waited a little before calling my mate again, hoping she would have it handy. When I reached her voicemail again, my level of anxiety surged. In all of our time together, Jade always answered my calls, no matter how busy she was, or at least texted to let me know she couldn't answer right now.

Wincing in pain, I crawled out of bed and stepped into the bathroom to wash the sleep from my face. I cringed at my reflection in the full mirror on the bathroom door. Despite my ethereal shield, Morgan had done a number on me, his shadowy tendrils imprinted all over my skin in shades of black, purple, and yellow.

After getting dressed, I checked my phone again; still no text message or call from Jade. Fighting the urge to take more meds, since the last dose had been too recent, I walked out of my bedroom into the living area. A dark shape on the floor by the entrance immediately drew my attention. I approached it to investigate, the sense of dread which gnawed at me rising exponentially as I recognized the black business card that had been slipped in through the door mail slot.

The front of the glossy black card simply displayed a stylized white text stating '4D' which I assumed stood for Fourth Division. The white matte back of the card contained two lines of text handwritten in black ink. The first read 'You broke the agreement' while the second indicated an address with simply a street name and door number.

For a moment, my vision blurred with blind fury. They'd

dared come to my home to take my woman under false pretenses. I hadn't breached any agreement, although when it came to protecting my mate, I would have without hesitation. If they thought to use their failure to ensure Jade's safety as an argument to keep us apart, they had another thing coming.

My first instinct was to call a cab, but then it struck me that their hand delivery of the card implied they'd likely apprehended Jade right here. Grabbing the second set of car keys, I headed down to the garage to have my suspicions confirmed with my car parked in its reserved spot. My anger flared further when I found the doors unlocked but no keys in the ignition. The bastards must have cornered her before she could even set her foot inside.

After entering the address into my car's integrated GPS, I drove off, relieved that the destination sat in the industrial sector of the city and not some remote, shady place where one would dump a body. Yet, something didn't add up. They'd clearly taken Jade as bait to lure me; a pretty dishonorable tactic that didn't fit with my reading of Agent Thomson. Our text conversation last night hadn't indicated any intent of litigating me over my killing Morgan. And even if he had, I believed Thomson would have first asked me to turn myself in, keeping Jade as an ultimate weapon in case all else failed.

While speeding down the highway, I wondered if I should have called Agent Thomson to ask why—and if—he'd pulled such a stunt. The more I thought about it, the more it felt like something Agent Wilkins would do. Thomson had kept him on a tight leash, but the younger agent held an obvious hatred of my kind that bordered on the fanatical because of what happened to his sister.

It struck me then that in my haste, I'd left my phone at home, not that it would have done me any good. Clearly, they'd taken Jade's phone away, and they had not bothered to call me. They didn't want a conversation but a confrontation.

Worst case scenario, I had just enough energy left to cross the

Veil back into the Mist, but not enough to preserve this body. I couldn't let things devolve into a fight, especially so far away from the next Mist. If I harmed any agent, they'd put me on the wanted list and seek to banish me by any means. This meant no more life with Jade as they'd have around the clock surveillance around her to catch me. With Laura in the picture, running away together wouldn't be an option. Conclusion: I needed to keep my cool and not be tricked into using my power.

As I pulled up to the parking lot of the dark building, which no doubt served as the Men in Black's headquarters, a single agent came out. My heart sank as I recognized Agent Thomson. Had I so badly misread him? Even now, as I parked in the spot closest to the entrance, ignoring the reserved sign, the emotions emanating from him contained no malice, only a hefty dose of worry and an underlying layer of anger that didn't feel aimed at me.

I got out of the car, slamming the door behind me. Thomson took a few steps towards me, raising his palms before him in an appeasing gesture.

"Mr. Dale," he called out as I continued my approach, "I'm sorry you had to come all the way here this morning. There's been a terrible misunderstanding."

"Where's my Jade?" I asked, stopping a few feet from him.

"Ms. Eastwood is inside, safe and unharmed," he said, gesturing towards the entrance. "I made sure of it. This should never have happened. It wasn't an authorized mission."

I narrowed my eyes at him, seeking any signs of duplicity, not wanting to give in to relief too soon.

"I promise you, Mr. Dale, I honor my deals. Unfortunately, one of our agents acted overzealously," Thomson said, no doubt sensing my hesitation.

"Wilkins," I said, my anger resurfacing.

Thomson's sigh and discouraged expression confirmed my guess. "As soon as we've settled this mess, I will put him on disciplinary leave and demand a psychological evaluation to assess his fitness for duty. I'm afraid dealing with Morgan's victims over the past week has pushed him over the fine line he was already treading."

I nodded curtly and gave him a challenging stare. "I want to see Jade."

"Of course." Agent Thomson turned slightly and gestured at the entrance. "This way, please."

"I didn't break the agreement," I said as we walked side by side towards the building.

My back stiffened at Thomson's hesitation.

"No, you didn't," the older man said, choosing his words carefully. "However, the more bigoted among the force say that, technically, you did since Morgan was in human form when you killed him, and the agreement was to not drain any human."

The tall glass doors opened automatically upon our approach. I scanned the large entrance hall for threats or signs of treachery. Empty but for a few benches along the dark grey walls and the reception desk in the middle, it held a solemn severity that naturally incited people to talk in hushed tones. The two security guards at the desk on a quiet Saturday morning screamed overkill, not to mention the half dozen other agents that conveniently happened to be idling within intervention range, pretending to be talking in pairs or looking at their phones. Yet, the not-so-subtle furtive glances in our direction weighed heavily upon me.

"His ashes would have confirmed his nature," I said absent-mindedly as I assessed the emotional state of the agents.

Fear and curiosity dominated among them, aside from one who reeked with distrust and borderline hatred. I turned my head towards him, staring him straight in the eyes.

"Hello," I said in a somewhat taunting tone.

The agent's eyes widened then he quickly averted them without answering.

Thomson frowned. "Please, do not provoke the men."

Although worded as a request, I didn't miss the underlying warning in his voice.

"I'm not provoking them but issuing a preemptive warning, letting him know that I'm on to him," I said with a shrug. "If he has ill intentions, he will not get the drop on me."

Thomson harrumphed noncommittally as we stepped into the elevator. It took us to an overly bright and clinically white hallway with doors on each side simply identified by a large letter and a two-digit number. Right outside the elevator, a man at a small security desk nodded for us to proceed after making eye contact with Agent Thomson.

The unpleasant sense of imminent doom returned as I wondered if I'd allowed myself to be lured to my execution. But the tingle associated with Jade's presence engulfed me. It grew stronger with each step we took forward. Impatience had me increasing the pace, forcing Thomson to accelerate as well. I didn't even care about his amused smirk, overwhelmed by the need to hold my mate. It became so strong that I didn't need the agent to indicate to me which room she was in. I half-ran to door E.27 and turned the handle only to find it locked.

Agent Thomson chuckled and waved his ID card in front of a security card reader on the wall that I'd failed to notice in my eagerness. The red LED on it turned green, and I immediately turned the handle again. I'd no sooner opened the door than Jade shouted my name.

My mate jumped to her feet from the chair she'd been sitting in and ran towards me. She threw herself into my arms, and I wrapped them tightly around her, oblivious to the pain from my bruises. Gripping my hair with both hands, she crushed my lips with a desperate kiss to which I responded in kind. Breaking the kiss, she buried her face in the crook of my neck and held me tightly. With one hand around her back and the other holding her nape, I kissed the top of her head before resting my cheek against it, inhaling deeply the familiar and soothing scent of the flowery shampoo she used.

Reluctantly releasing her, I examined her face and body for any sign of injury. She giggled, telling me she was fine. Lifting my head, I noticed the agent at the back of the room who'd been standing guard. He looked familiar as he stared at us with a troubled look on his face. It took me a moment to remember seeing him at the gallery last night. This explained how they'd been so quickly on site to clean things up.

His emotions broadcast surprise, confusion, and blossoming doubt.

He thought me to be a monster like Morgan.

"I would like to take my woman home and for you to give me your assurance such a *misunderstanding* will not occur again," I said to Agent Thomson in a stern tone.

"Naturally," Thomson said in a conciliatory voice. "However, as Ms. Eastwood didn't witness your encounter with the Nightmare, I would need to record your deposition. Agent Tate here will bear witness. It shouldn't be more than twenty minutes of your time, and then you can be off and not have to see us again."

Although reluctant, I cast an inquisitive look at Jade who nodded her assent. With a sigh, I sat in the chair Thomson indicated and then pulled my woman onto my lap. She snuggled against me, and I absentmindedly caressed her fiery hair. Agent Tate placed the recorder on the table before me and turned it on. As I spoke, the sense of unease returned. I tried to keep it short, but Agent Thomson asked me to specify every time he felt I was cutting corners. Just as I got to the part where I'd asked Monica to call the chauffeur to take Jade and me home, the door of the interrogation room burst open.

Startled, we all turned to find Wilkins and two other agents walking into the room, one of them the agent that had exuded hatred in the main hall upon my arrival. All senses on full alert, I made Jade stand up, rose to my feet as well, and then pushed her behind me. The three new agents immediately placed their hands on their holsters, ready to draw their weapons.

Agent Thomson and Agent Tate jumped to their feet.

"What the fuck are you doing here, Wilkins?" Thomson snapped. "I told you to wait in my office to face disciplinary measures."

"As per the rules," Wilkins said with a malicious smile, "I am not obligated to follow the orders of a superior who has been compromised."

"Me, compromised?" Agent Thomson asked, bewildered.

The flicker of unease in Agent Tate's eyes, and the torn emotions emanating from him indicated we might find an ally in him.

"You are single handedly trying to exonerate a serial killer in breach of agreement who is also spreading propaganda with the aid of his accomplice to incite women to commit suicide," Wilkins said pointing an angry finger at Jade on the last word.

"Serial Killer? You are insane," Thomson whispered, looking at his partner like he was seeing him for the first time.

Beyond insane.

"I am *not* insane," Wilkins snapped taking a step forward.

Pushing Jade further away, I also took a step back then prepared to raise my ethereal shield if needed.

"The killer's energy signature found on most of the thirteen victims from this week is similar to the one found on the gallery corpse this monster claims was Morgan," Wilkins said, pointing at me.

"Similar doesn't mean same or identical," Thomson said, waving a dismissive hand. "The similarity is normal considering they both sparked from Ms. Eastwood."

"That still doesn't prove the carcass we found belonged to Morgan," Wilkins argued, his face taking on a mulish expression.

"His ashes do," I countered.

"There were no ashes with the corpse," Wilkins said. "The pile we found was quite far from it."

"Because I hid the corpse to prevent humans from stumbling upon it," I said, my voice clearly indicating how stupid I found that comment.

"These could have been the ashes from anyone, not necessarily your victim's," he argued.

I shrugged. "DNA would prove—"

"You can't get DNA from ashes, you dumbass," Wilkins interrupted.

Okay, I hadn't known that.

"But you can compare the corpse's DNA to the blood found in my house after Morgan attacked me," Jade said from behind me.

"And they did match," Thomson confirmed, his voice filled with tension.

"That still doesn't prove that Morgan wasn't human," Wilkins said.

"What?" Jade and I exclaimed at the same time.

"For all we know," Wilkins said, staring at Jade with disdain, "you were fucking that man, too, got into a lover's spat, and used us and your demon to settle the score. It wouldn't be the first time some sick bitch abused the law to get revenge."

"You tread carefully, human," I hissed, taking a threatening step towards the son of a bitch.

"Or what, demon? You're going to leech me too?" Wilkins taunted.

"Mr. Dale, please," Agent Thomson cautioned.

I reined in the urge to slaughter Wilkins, knowing he was trying to goad me into doing something that would justify violent action. Jade's delicate hand rubbing my back soothingly helped greatly.

"I assure you," I said in a barely controlled voice, "it was no human I battled last night."

Lifting my shirt off, I held it fisted in my hand. All the agents in the room gasped, eyes wide at the sight of the bruises covering my body.

"Rather than harassing us, you should be getting on your knees and thanking me for permanently taking out that Nightmare. If not for my ethereal powers, he would have crushed me to a pulp. Against one of you, each of these blows would have punched right through flesh and bones, splitting you in half."

An uneasy silence followed my words.

"You've seen it," I whispered, understanding dawning on me at the haunted looks in the men's eyes.

"Yes," Thomson said, grimly. "Five of the thirteen victims this week were agents."

I flinched. No wonder they'd displayed so much hatred and resentment towards my kind.

"Oh God," Jade whispered.

"God has nothing to do with it," Wilkins said, snapping out of his haunted daze, the insane glimmer in his eyes shining brighter than ever. "This is why we need to eliminate these abominations," he said, flicking open the safety latch of his holster. "These demons should not be here, infesting our world and corrupting our women. He must return to Hell where he belongs, and that bitch needs to be indicted for heinous propaganda."

"That's enough, Jeff!" Agent Thomson said, his own hand hovering over his hip before realizing he didn't have a weapon, being in civilian clothes. "I'm relieving you of duty and putting you on administrative leave until you've completed a psychological evaluation to determine your ability to serve. Gentlemen, please seize him."

The two agents who had walked into the room with Wilkins hesitated. While I could still sense their hatred towards my kind, and therefore me, they were starting to realize that their leader had gone off the deep end. That hesitation was enough to create the opportunity the crazy man needed.

Whipping out his gun, Wilkins aimed at Agent Thomson. Everyone tensed, the other agents pulling out their own weapons but not seeming to know where to aim.

"I'm relieving *you* of duty, Agent Thomson. It is obvious that your extensive exposure to these unnatural beings has tainted your perception of right and wrong and made you forget your oath to protect humans first."

"Jefferson," Thomson said, raising his palms in an appeasing gesture, "put down your weapon, son. Don't throw away your life and your career. Let's talk about this."

"We can talk after I've sent this demon back to Hell."

My shield went up half a second before he finished turning his weapon towards me. Still, the bullet struck the center of my chest with the force of a freight train, knocking the wind out of me. Despite my vision blurring from the pain, I lunged at him through the shouts of the men and Jade's horrified scream. With an angry roar, I grabbed his hands and pinned them against the wall to prevent him from shooting again. In my current state, I couldn't handle too many more.

"Get off me!" Wilkins shouted, trying to break free of my hold. I pressed my body to his to keep him from kicking and kneeing me. "Shoot him!"

"Don't shoot!" Thomson yelled.

Time stood still for a moment then an evil glimmer of clarity flashed through Wilkins' eyes, sending a cold shiver down my spine.

"Help! He's leeching me! Kill him! KILL HIM!"

Multiple deflagrations deafened me followed immediately by the atrocious pain of two bullets battering my ethereal shield along my right leg. The third pierced through it, and I cried out in agony as my femur shattered under the close range impact. I stumbled backwards before collapsing onto the floor. Through blurred vision I watched helplessly as Wilkins aimed his gun at my chest with a demented grin on his face. Through the blood rushing in my ears, I heard the men's panicked shouts, Thomson yelling warnings at Wilkins to stop, and Jade screaming my name. The latter affected me the most; I couldn't console or protect her.

I should have taken her home when I had the chance.

As if in slow motion, a bright flash appeared at the muzzle of Wilkins' gun followed by a golden bullet racing towards me. Just as it buried itself in my chest, three holes appeared in the middle of Wilkins' own chest, his pristine, white dress shirt greedily absorbing his life's blood. He stared at his wounds with a surprised expression before sliding down the wall, his eyes glazing over.

The most horrible pain I'd ever felt tore me apart as the bullet shattered inside of me. My heart stuttered while my lungs filled with liquid I could only assume to be blood. The room spun around me, the cold tiles beneath my bare back feeling warmer than my own body.

"KAZAN!" Jade screamed, rushing to my side and falling to her knees next to me.

Tuning out the chaos all around us, I struggled to focus on my beautiful Jade's face. Strained with sorrow, her cheeks drenched with tears, she looked at me with pleading eyes.

"Don't leave me. Please, don't leave me," she begged, shaking her head in denial.

"My Jade," I said, my mouth filling with blood.

I tried to raise a hand to caress her face but didn't have the strength. Jade took my hand and brought it to her cheek, leaning into it. Her pain tortured me far worse than my failing vessel.

"Please, baby. Please," she begged.

"I have loved you my whole life," I said, my voice wet from

the blood filling my lungs. "I will always love you, in this world and all others beyond. Thank you for wishing me."

"No, Kazan. No! I love you. You can't leave me." She looked up at the men around us. "Help him, please. Please!"

Cracks appeared on my hand pressed against her cheek and along my arm like it would on dried mud. Part of my hand as well as lumps of flesh along my arms crumbled into ashes as I felt myself float away.

"Jade," I whispered, before the last of my consciousness was sucked away into the void under the fading sound of my one true love's agonized scream of despair.

CHAPTER 13

JADE

K azan was dead; permanently dead. Even as his body had turned to ashes in my arms, I'd held on to the belief that, somehow, he'd return to me. After his men had disposed of Wilkins' body, Agent Thomson did his best to console me and offered to have his people handle Kazan's funeral. Either way, because of his fame, they had to spin an acceptable tale to avoid suspicion. I didn't give a shit about suspicion or 'protecting the public' kind of bullshit. My heart had been torn right out of my chest with his passing.

Ultimately, I convinced Agent Thomson to keep Kazan's death a secret. He'd promised to always fight for me. He'd traveled across worlds to be with me. I refused to believe this was it. The news crushed Monica. In some ways, my loss made her relive hers. As much as it shamed me to have her go through this again, she was my rock through this nightmare.

Kazan shouldn't have died. Even though the first shots would have left him with a permanent limp, the other agents had not shot to kill, only to incapacitate. Crazy or not, I felt no sympathy for Wilkins. If Agent Tate hadn't killed him, I would have. How ironic that his former partner in crime should have been the one to put him down once he'd realized who the true monster in the room was.

The twenty-six days before the first Mist after his death dragged on at an excruciatingly slow pace. Over the three days it lasted, my heart broke even more as my hopes and prayers remained unanswered; Kazan didn't visit me.

As soon as the Mist lifted, I visited every location he had shown me in the Mist as the places he used for birthing his human form and where he used to stash whatever he owned to give him a leg up on his next incarnation. But that, too, proved another crushing disappointment. At the end of the third month, with still no signs from Kazan, I had no choice but to give in to both Agent Thomson's and Monica's pressure to announce Kazan's death and give him an official burial.

We obviously couldn't give him an open casket funeral even though the Fourth Division had done an amazing job of preserving him. Still, with the parts of him that had turned to ash, he looked like a chipped and partially broken statue. Monica accompanied me when the agents cremated his remains. Laura had wanted to attend to support me, but the Fourth Division didn't allow it.

Monica took care of the public funeral. There was an impressive attendance from fans and other members of the artistic community. They all commiserated with me and mourned the senseless loss of such a talented man to a landslide while driving along a hilly area.

The week after, I found out that Kazan had declared me his sole heir and executor. His will had been drawn up around the time Patrick and I had considered getting married. His wealth exceeded what I could make in a lifetime in my current career. Yet, I would have given it all up for a chance to be with him again.

Despite all that, I kept clinging to hope. I remembered Kazan saying he would gather energy for five to six months to be able to stay in my world without an anchor for a few weeks. When the sixth month came and went and I didn't find him at any of his locations, I finally accepted that he was gone.

I'd been living in Kazan's flat since his death to feel his presence around me but, under both my sister and Monica's advice, I sold both the apartment and my house. I'd been on sabbatical from work since that tragic day but decided to hand in my resignation. After packing my belongings and the six centerpiece paintings of us, I donated Kazan's clothes to homeless shelters, left town, and moved into a cozy little house near my sister's college. Not knowing what I wanted to do with the rest of my empty life, I was happy the landlord had agreed to rent it as I didn't want to commit to anything at this point.

As the City Defense Alarm sounded outside, I slowly walked to the closed window and watch the Mist rise, gradually drowning the city in its white vapor. I no longer feared it, knowing its rules and inhabitants. Still, as the outline of the first lumbering silhouette of a Mistbeast appeared in the distance, I activated the metal shutters, having no desire to gaze upon other people's nightmares.

I had enough of my own.

EPILOGUE
KAZAN

C old. Biting cold. Numb fingers, hands, and feet. Even my blood felt on the verge of turning to ice in my veins. Turning to my side left me exhausted and panting for breath. But the freezing air stabbed at my lungs and airways.

I'm too weak. This was too soon.

But it had been so long… Would my impatience be my ultimate demise? Even opening my eyes felt like a herculean feat. When I did, the sight before me gave my lurching heart a jolt. Less than a meter away on a low bench, folded and protected from mold and humidity by a plastic bag, a thick blanket stared at me.

I hadn't left it there. In fact, I had neglected my birth refuge since I'd met Jade. Had someone else begun using it? Still, the prospect of warmth gave me a surge of strength. Rolling to my stomach, I struggled to get to all fours, my arms and legs shaking. Advancing at a snail's pace with ungainly movements, I finally reached my target. Too numb, my fingers barely managed to get my prize out of its wrapping. A strangled moan tore from my throat as the blessed heat of the blanket settled over me.

A white, rectangular-shaped object dangling from a corner of the blanket drew my attention. Reaching for it with trembling hands, I lifted it closer to my face and nearly wept realizing it was a controller for a battery-operated heating blanket. I pressed the ON button and within seconds, the temperature of the blanket increased. I moaned with pleasure, wrapping myself tightly in this heavenly gift, and curled up into a fetal position.

I don't know how long I stayed like that, gradually feeling warm and toasty, my newborn body coming back to life. The City Defense Alarm, sounding off in the distance, prompted me out of my cocoon. Standing on unsteady feet, I frowned at the sight of a large suitcase next to the waterproof storage cabinet I'd brought here. A note inside a transparent plastic cover had been taped on top.

Leaning forward, my throat tightened and my chest constricted as I began reading.

'Dear Traveler,

May these items provide you the strength and comfort required to pursue your wish, as I'd hoped they would my Kazan.

J.'

My Jade... My beautiful Jade... Even after she'd lost hope for us, she would help others achieve their dreams. My heart filled to bursting as I opened the suitcase to find warm clothes, boots to my size, a winter coat, a wallet containing two hundred dollars, and a disposable phone. Tears pricked my eyes as I put on the divine clothes. They were a little big, but I didn't care.

Opening the storage cabinet, my heart soared once more with gratitude to find it filled with bottles of water, cans of energy drinks, energy bars, beef jerky and various other consumables with long expiration dates. Sitting on the low bench, I downed an energy drink. To my pleasant surprise, this body didn't seem to mind the excessive sugar it contained. Nevertheless, I washed it away with a bottle of water before chewing on an energy bar. As I started on the second one, ready to open the package of the disposable phone, the sound of an approaching car startled me.

Rising to my feet, I listened, heart pounding as the car stopped outside the shed that sheltered me, and the driver killed the engine. Standing at the ready, I braced for who would enter. As much as I wished it would be Jade, from her dreams, I knew she wouldn't come here anymore, having decided to force herself to move on.

The door opened on the broad silhouette of a man. The brightness of early morning light flooding into the windowless shack blinded me. I hadn't realize just how dark it had been in here. I blinked, trying to make out the face of the intruder.

Or was it of the owner?

"Welcome back, Mistwalker," said a familiar, deep voice.

"Agent Thomson!" I whispered.

"You certainly took your time coming back to your woman," he said, in a slightly chastising tone.

I gaped at him, speechless.

He smiled then lifted the heavy bag in his hand, showing it to me. "Well, I guess you won't need this, after all. Someone already took care of you," he said, giving my outfit a meaningful glance.

"You knew," I said, my voice throaty for lack of use.

"Energy surge, remember?" he said with a teasing tone. He gave me a once over, an approving glimmer in his eyes. "Body upgrade? Smart decision."

Looking down at myself, my face heated slightly.

"Some might consider it a downgrade," I said, having chosen a different body this time, a little shorter and less massive.

"But more normal, although still on the tall and muscular side," the agent said. "The slight facial changes will also make our lives easier."

Coming closer, Agent Thomson emptied the contents of his

bag into the suitcase, leaving warm clothes, a coat, and a pair of boots.

"You might as well put the money and phone back in there," the agent said, "you won't need them." He smiled at my worried but curious look. "I'm taking you home to your woman."

Emotion threatened to overwhelm me again. Before finding the disposable phone, I had dreaded the long walk back to civilization in the snow and cold winds. After finding it, I had planned on calling Monica, hoping she would believe it was me, to ask her to pick me up. Not knowing how Jade would react, I didn't want to unnecessarily traumatize her.

"Thank you, Agent Thomson," I said with sincere gratitude.

"Alfred. Call me Alfred, Fred, or Al," the agent said, his laugh lines crinkling. "This isn't Fourth Division business. Just don't mention to anyone that I've used their systems to find you." Worry must have shown in my face, making his smile broaden. "Relax, son, I've deleted the record of your energy surge from our systems."

My shoulders sagged with relief.

"Thank you, Al," I said with a sheepish smile. "You can call me Kazan."

"No," Alfred said, in a tone that brooked no argument. "Kazan Dale died four months ago from a tragic landslide while he drove through a hilly countryside. Hundreds of people mourned his death and attended his funeral."

Pulling a small wallet from his pocket, he tossed it towards me. I caught it and flipped it open to find a couple of ID cards, including social security and birth certification cards.

"You are now Kyle Winters." Chuckling at my dismay, he gestured towards the door with his head. "Come on, let's get out of here."

I followed in his wake, eager to be reunited with my mate. Despite the warm coat, the cold, early morning air nipped at me during the short walk to the car. Looking at the long, deserted road ahead, it became clear to me that I never would have made it. Thomson fired the engine as I buckled my seatbelt. No doubt sensing my heavy stare on him, he turned to give me a quizzical look.

"I don't know why you are doing this, but from the bottom of my heart, I thank you," I said, not knowing how else to express the depth of my gratitude.

The older man's expression softened. For the first time, I experienced what I believed a father's indulgent gaze upon his son would feel like. Al didn't answer right away. Instead, he picked up a tall, insulated cup from the cup holder in the car and extended it to me.

"Chicken broth," Al said. "Should still be hot, so be careful not to burn yourself."

I gladly accepted the offering, welcoming the warmth of the container between my fingers.

"There are a couple of BLT sandwiches in that bag," he added, indicating with his chin a brown bag in the console between our seats. "I heard they were your favorite," he explained at my stunned expression.

Silence stretched for a moment as he turned onto the main road. I didn't press him, sensing he needed time to decide how to answer my implied question.

"I have a daughter, Giselle. She's about the same age as Ms. Eastwood," Al said in a conversational tone, his eyes on the road. "Since her teenage years, she's been an endless source of worry. She was a good girl but the biggest magnet for bad men. My baby would go from one abusive relationship to the next, one of which almost killed her."

"I'm sorry," I said.

Al shrugged. "Don't be. It wasn't your fault, but mine for not seeing how bad things had gotten for her. She'd come to my house for an early dinner, distressed that her ex had died in prison in some brawl with another inmate. That night changed everything. She left in time to make it home before the sirens went off. I'd just locked down my house for the Mist and went to my office to work on a new miniature airplane, as is my routine during those three days." His face tensed, and his jaw clenched as he reminisced. "I found Giselle's suicide note on my desk, begging for my forgiveness, but that she couldn't take the pain anymore."

My chest tightened for him, already guessing where this was headed.

"With the Mist having already come up, I couldn't get to Giselle's place. I called, and she didn't answer. It crushed me. My wife died years ago from breast cancer. My little girl was all I had left. But then, two hours later, she called me saying a Mist-walker outside her house had forced her to go back inside because it wasn't safe."

My heart warmed. "Her Wish," I said.

Agent Thomson nodded. "Over the next six months, he took her to your world during the Mist and brought her back before the alarm went off." He gave me a side glance full of emotion before returning his eyes to the road. "I'd never seen my daughter so happy. The inevitable happened. Risul couldn't handle mortal life, so she followed him into the Mist. I buried my daughter a little over eight years ago. Yet, every month, I spend the three days of the Mist with them, either in your world or here."

"I am very happy for you and your daughter," I said after swallowing another sip of the delicious broth. "It warms my heart that they found each other."

The agent smiled. "It took me no time to recognize that you were like him, merely trying to make some other man's daughter happy, like Risul had done for mine. But Nightmares are all that agents remember. Please don't judge us too harshly."

"I don't. I understand all too well what ravages a single

Nightmare can cause." Tilting my head, I gave him a questioning look. "You encounter many of them every Mist?"

Agent Thomson snorted. "No. They're extremely rare. Very few of your kind crossover. Among those who do, many die within the first couple of days, too weak or clueless to adapt to our world. You were smart," he said, giving a side glance full of respect. "You carefully planned your arrival in a safe birth place. You have no idea how many of your peers get devoured by Mist-beasts halfway through forming their human shell. In truth, Men in Black is a rather pompous title for the cleanup crew. After the Mist, we mostly spend our time disposing of the remains of Beasts and Walkers who failed to get back through the Veil, dealing with missing persons, Mist Pacts, or false Mist tragedies used to hide domestic homicides."

"I'm sorry for that," I said. "But that there are so few Night-mares is a relief."

He nodded. "It is. If not for that Nightmare, you'd have been the most exciting thing to have happened to the department in a few years. Now that Kazan Dale is no more, how about a career in the Fourth Division? We could use a Hunter like you."

I snorted. "No thanks. I'm definitely not a monster hunter. Jade wouldn't permit it anyway."

"Figures," he said, with a mocking smile.

"I'm sorry about your partner," I said, abruptly changing the topic.

Thomson sighed and shook his head at the wasted life.

"Don't be. He'd been losing it for a while. I'm just sorry you and Ms. Eastwood had to suffer so much for it. At least, that incident has forced us to revise our process for emotional and psychological evaluation of the agents frequently exposed to stress situations."

I was about to answer when I noticed we weren't heading towards City Center but away from town. My head jerked towards him, not wanting to believe he could be betraying me.

"Relax, son," Thomson said, having noticed my unease. "After your funeral, Ms. Eastwood moved to Covington to be closer to her sister. But before I take you there, we need to make a slight detour to one of our safe houses so that we can get some official pictures of you for your remaining IDs; passport, driver's license, etc."

Twenty-five minutes after leaving my birth shed, we reached an inconspicuous looking little house in a quiet neighborhood. Agent Thomson... Al... made me shower, fix my disheveled hair, and put on a black sweater better fitted to my new size before we took the pictures. I actually welcomed the opportunity to make myself a bit more presentable before seeing Jade again.

I hope she will like this new body.

It took the agent thirty minutes to finish assembling my IDs, and then another twenty-minute drive before we reached Jade's quaint little stone cottage. My pulse pounded into my throat as I looked at the shuttered windows, knowing the love of my life was inside, only meters away from me.

"This is your new start, Mr. Winters," Al said, extending me a folder. "Your name doesn't appear in any Fourth Division file. To us, you are just another law-abiding citizen, born of human parents. I hope we never meet again."

Throat constricted, I nodded and shook his hand. "I hope we never meet again in this world, but maybe we'll cross paths in the Mist."

The older man smiled, becoming paternal again. "Maybe. Now go on and make your woman happy. She's waited a long time for you."

Swallowing hard, I nodded again and got out of the car. The crunching sound of freshly fallen snow under my boots drowned beneath the erratic beating of my heart as I walked up to the door. In spite of the cold air stabbing at my lungs, I took a deep, fortifying breath before ringing the bell.

My body thrumming with trepidation, I feared for a moment

that she'd still be fast asleep. Jade slept like the dead. No amount of ringing would have wakened her. When the shutters began to rise, my heart leapt in my chest.

The inner wooden door opened slightly, Jade's magnificent green eyes peeking through the narrow slit. They widened in shock. I held my breath as she opened it wide, her hand clutching my brand over the silky, green robe covering her nightgown. Her lips quivered, and her body trembled as she stared at me through the screen door.

"My Jade," I whispered.

"Kazan," she mouthed.

Something caught Jade's eyes, and she peered behind me. Looking over my shoulder, I watched Agent Thomson raise a hand in farewell, then drive off. I turned back to Jade to find her fumbling with the lock. I took a step back as she pushed the door open. Taking a couple of steps forward, I stopped on the threshold of her house where I stood transfixed before her.

"You came back," she whispered. "You came back."

"I will always come back to you, Jade. I have crossed the Veil a hundred times to be with you. Nothing, not even death, can keep us apart."

Tears of joy filled her eyes as she extended her arms towards me. "My Kazan," she said, smiling through her tears.

Her blessing received, I stepped over the threshold and pulled her into my arms. Our lips found each other's. Wrapped in the divine emotions of my beloved, I knew that this time, my journey had ended. I was home.

JADE

E ven six years after that most improbable day when Kazan —correction, Kyle—returned to me, I never tired of gazing on the perfection that was my man. His new body had taken a bit of getting used to. Six-foot-four instead of six-foot-seven had significantly improved his quality of life and made my own neck happier now that I no longer needed to crank it all the way back to look up at him.

Although I'd loved his old bodybuilder, barbarian-warrior, bulging muscles self, this book-cover-model-I-want-to-lick-those-crazy-abs new body was exactly what I'd truly, secretly wanted. While still sharing quite a few similarities with his old face, this one was more manly handsome and less boyishly pretty than the previous. With his black hair and the same stormy grey eyes I'd loved so much, he could have passed for Kazan's brother or relative.

After our steamy reunion, I'd berated him for not contacting me sooner during the Mist. Turns out we'd spent all these months together in my dreams, which I would immediately forget in the morning. He'd been too weak upon his return to his realm to draw me in during the Mist.

It had freaked me out to learn that after his death, he'd barely made it back to his realm. The sliver of him remaining had been barely stronger than a spark; a newborn Wish. He'd spent the first three months hiding from stronger Mist beings intent on feeding off of him while he personally hunted flickering Wishes that hadn't achieved self-awareness and therefore didn't flee in the presence of predators. By the start of the fourth month, he was strong enough to begin taking on lesser beasts. By the sixth, he'd been back to his old self. He only spent one month building his reserves after those six months of healing. Going through mortal birth at the seventh month had been reckless.

Still, I couldn't thank enough whatever powers allowed him to survive his ordeal and for letting him return to me.

While part of Kazan's ethereal form had turned to ashes upon his death—hence his weakened state back in the Mist—he explained that most of the ashes that had crumbled around him had actually resulted from Morgan's life force, which he had sucked in the night prior.

Walking up to my man seated on a stool as he worked, I ran my fingers through his raven hair, admiring his latest piece. With Kazan's death, Kyle couldn't pursue his career where he had left off. Instead of hyper realistic paintings, he took on hyper realistic sculpting. If not for the monster love theme of his pieces, he'd give Ron Mueck a run for his money.

"It's stunning," I whispered, as he put the final touches to the life-size sculpture of a naked woman in the loving embrace of a werewolf, breastfeeding a newborn child wrapped in a red cloak, with two little half-human, half-wolf pups leaning on each side of their father and trying to peek at their young sibling. "It's got to be my favorite"

He chuckled and wrapped an arm around my waist, drawing me to him. "You say that with every new piece. I thought the scaly alien with horns was your favorite."

"He is, too! It's your fault if I'm confused. Each of your pieces surpasses the others!" I exclaimed before kissing the top of his head.

"Why, thank you, my love," Kyle said, beaming at me. "Is that your way of saying you want to play with the wolf tonight?"

I felt myself blush and a swarm of butterflies took off in the pit of my stomach. "Maybe? I haven't seen that bushy tail in a while," I said coyly, leaning in to kiss him.

"Mommy! Mommy! Aunt Laura is here!" the shrill voice of our daughter screamed, startling me before my lips could even touch my husband's.

The stampeding sound of our children's little feet increased in volume as they came racing into the studio.

"Slow down, you little hellions!" I exclaimed as they came

barreling towards us. "What did I say about coming inside the studio?" I asked in a stern voice.

"No running," said Matt, my youngest, although it sounded more like 'wunning.' He scrunched up his adorable, three-year-old face, so similar to his father's.

"No fighting and no throwing stuff at my infur... insafu..."

"Insufferable," I said on her behalf.

"Yes! Insufable little brother," Serena said, making a face at him.

Kyle and I chuckled. He rose to his feet and, together, we went to greet my sister who'd babysit the children for us while we made sure to replenish my husband's ethereal reserves.

The City Defense Alarm went off just as we finished dinner.

"Oooh, can we open the shutters and watch the Beasts?" Matt asked, his stormy eyes pleading.

"No!" Serena shouted, turning identical grey eyes towards her sibling, one year younger than she.

"You know it gives your sister nightmares," Kyle said, reprovingly.

Matt stared at his sister, eyes full of mischief, then started making clucking sounds.

"You little...!"

Serena sprang out of her chair to chase after her brother, but Kyle caught her on the fly, drawing her to his lap.

"You two keep fighting, and we won't take you to the Mist," Kyle said, a warning in his voice.

Both children gasped and babbled almost in unison, begging to come and promising to be good.

"We'll take you to the Mist tomorrow night *IF* Aunt Laura tells us you've behaved all day," I said, trying to keep a severe expression on my face as I looked at my little demons.

For all the pranks and teasing, my children loved each other.

A couple of hours later, with our children bathed, teeth brushed, and tucked into their beds, we read them a bedtime story before kissing them goodnight. Ignoring Laura's suggestive wink as I wished her goodnight as well, I let my husband lead me by the hand to our bedroom.

Moments later, I found myself running through the Mist-filled woods of the dream world, naked but for my red, hooded cape, chased by a hungry wolf intent on capturing me. My heart pounded at the sound of his steps closing in on me, eager to claim his most willing prize.

He caught me, pinning me to the soft ground covered by cushion-like moss.

"Foolish girl," he growled, "you shouldn't have entered my domain. Now, I'm going to ravish and then devour you."

"Do your worst, beast!"

"I am no beast," he purred in his rumbling voice, before licking the brand over my exposed breast. "I am the monster in the Mist."

My monster. My Kazan. My greatest Wish.

THE END

ALSO BY REGINE ABEL

THE VEREDIAN CHRONICLES
Escaping Fate
Blind Fate
Raising Amalia
Twist of Fate
Hands of Fate
Defying Fate

BRAXIANS
Anton's Grace
Ravik's Mercy
Krygor's Hope

XIAN WARRIORS
Doom
Legion
Raven
Bane
Chaos
Varnog
Reaper
Wrath
Xenon
Nevrik

PRIME MATING AGENCY
I Married A Lizardman
I Married A Naga
I Married A Birdman
I Married A Minotaur
I Married A Merman

I Married A Dragon
I Married A Beast
I Married A Dryad

THE MIST
The Mistwalker
The Nightmare

DARK TALES
Bluebeard's Curse
The Hunchback

BLOOD MAIDENS OF KARTHIA
Claiming Thalia

VALOS OF SONHADRA
Unfrozen
Iced

EMPATHS OF LYRIA
An Alien For Christmas

THE SHADOW REALMS
Dark Swan

OTHER
True As Steel
Alien Awakening
Heart of Stone

ABOUT REGINE

USA Today bestselling author Regine Abel is a fantasy, paranormal and sci-fi junkie. Anything with a bit of magic, a touch of the unusual, and a lot of romance will have her jumping for joy. She loves creating hot alien warriors and no-nonsense, kick-ass heroines that evolve in fantastic new worlds while embarking on action-packed adventures filled with mystery and the twists you never saw coming.

Before devoting herself as a full-time writer, Regine had surrendered to her other passions: music and video games! After a decade working as a Sound Engineer in movie dubbing and live concerts, Regine became a professional Game Designer and Creative Director, a career that has led her from her home in Canada to the US and various countries in Europe and Asia.

Facebook
https://www.facebook.com/regine.abel.author/

Website
https://regineabel.com

Regine's Rebels Reader Group
https://www.facebook.com/groups/ReginesRebels/

Newsletter
http://smarturl.it/RA_Newsletter

Goodreads
http://smarturl.it/RA_Goodreads

Bookbub
https://www.bookbub.com/profile/regine-abel

Amazon
http://smarturl.it/AuthorAMS